"The untamed landscape is reflected in the wilderness of the human heart. Hitchcock shows us that it's possible to survive the crossings between wealthy and impoverished, indigenous and settler, proving that any line that divides can just as easily bind."

—Anne Keala Kelly (Kanaka ʻŌiwi), filmmaker and journalist

"The Alaskan answer to *The House on Mango Street*, with full, round portraits presented with poetry, grace, and insight."

—David Cheezem, Fireside Books, Palmer, AK

"This is a novel of second chances, of teens being teens, and of what it meant to be the first generation of youth in Alaska to experience statehood. Truly universal."

—Kari Meutsch, Phoenix Books, Burlington and Essex, VT

"A thoughtful, realistic novel about community, both the one you are born into, and the one you can create."

—Erin Barker, Hooray for Books!, Alexandria, VA

"As Sherman Alexie and Louise Erdrich showed readers life on Native American reservations, now Bonnie-Sue Hitchcock shares the lives of native and white inhabitants of Alaska shortly after it became a state. Poignant and heart-wrenching."

—Danielle Borsch, Vroman's Bookstore, Pasadena, CA

The Smell
of Other People's Houses

THE
SMELL
—OF—
OTHER
PEOPLE'S
HOUSES

*Bonnie-Sue
Hitchcock*

WENDY
LAMB
BOOKS

Text copyright © 2016 by Bonnie-Sue Hitchcock
Jacket art copyright © 2016 by Getty Images
Interior illustrations copyright © 2016 by Rebecca Poulson
Map copyright © 2016 by Kayley Lefaiver

Grateful acknowledgment is made to the following for permission to reprint previously published material:
Chandonnet, Ann: Lines from "In the Cranberry Gardens" from *Ptarmigan Valley: Poems of Alaska* by Ann Chandonnet. Reprinted by permission of Ann Chandonnet. Straley, John: *Haikus* by John Straley. Reprinted by permission of John Straley. White Carlstrom, Nancy: Lines from "Sun at the Top of the World" from *Midnight Dance of the Snowshoe Hare* by Nancy White Carlstrom. Reprinted by permission of Nancy White Carlstrom.

A previous version of the title chapter was published as Fast Fiction in the *Los Angeles Review,* Volume 18, Fall 2012.

Visit us on the Web! randomhouseteens.com

Educators and librarians, for a variety of teaching tools, visit us at RHTeachersLibrarians.com

Library of Congress Cataloging-in-Publication Data
Hitchcock, Bonnie-Sue
The smell of other people's houses / Bonnie-Sue Hitchcock. — First edition.
pages cm
Summary: "Growing up in Alaska in the 1970s isn't like growing up anywhere else: Don't think life is going to be easy. Know your place. And never talk about yourself. Four vivid voices tell intertwining stories of hardship, tragedy, wild luck, and salvation"—Provided by publisher.
ISBN 978-0-553-49778-6 (trade) — ISBN 978-0-553-49779-3 (lib. bdg.) — ISBN 978-0-553-49781-6 (pbk.) — ISBN 978-0-553-49780-9 (ebook) 1. Alaska—History—20th century—Juvenile fiction. [1. Alaska—History—20th century—Fiction. 2. Friendship—Fiction.] I. Title.
PZ7.1.H58Sm 2016
[Fic]—dc23
2015011309

The text of this book is set in 12-point Apollo.
Jacket design by Ray Shappell
Interior design by Trish Parcell

Printed in the United States of America
10 9 8 7 6 5 4 3 2 1
First Edition

For Gramzy

Cast of Key Characters
(roughly in order of introduction; narrators in boldface)

IN FAIRBANKS, ALASKA

Ruth
Mama
Daddy
Lily: Ruth's younger sister
Gran
Ray
Dumpling
Bunny: Lily's best friend,
  Dumpling's younger sister
Selma: Ruth's best friend
Alyce: Selma's cousin
Dora: Dumpling's best friend
Bumpo: Dora's dad
Mr. Moses: Dumpling's dad

Dora
Crazy Dancing Guy
Mom
Dumpling's mother
Paula and Annette: Mom's
  friends
George: cashier at the Salvation
  Army

IN SOUTHEAST ALASKA
AND CANADA

Alyce
Mom
Dad
Aunt Abigail: Selma's mother
Uncle Gorky

Hank
Sam: Hank's younger brother
Jack: Hank's youngest brother
Mom
Nathan: Mom's boyfriend
Phil: night watchman on the
  ferry
Isabelle: social worker

Ruth
Abbess
Sister Agnes
Sister Bernadette
Sister Josephine

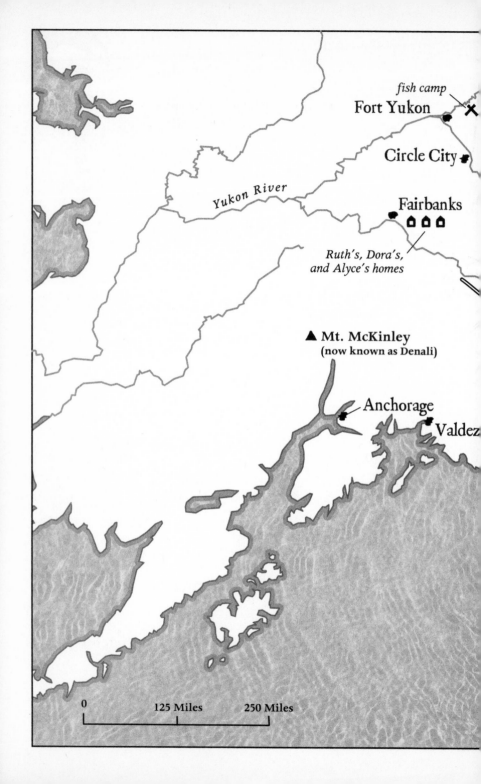

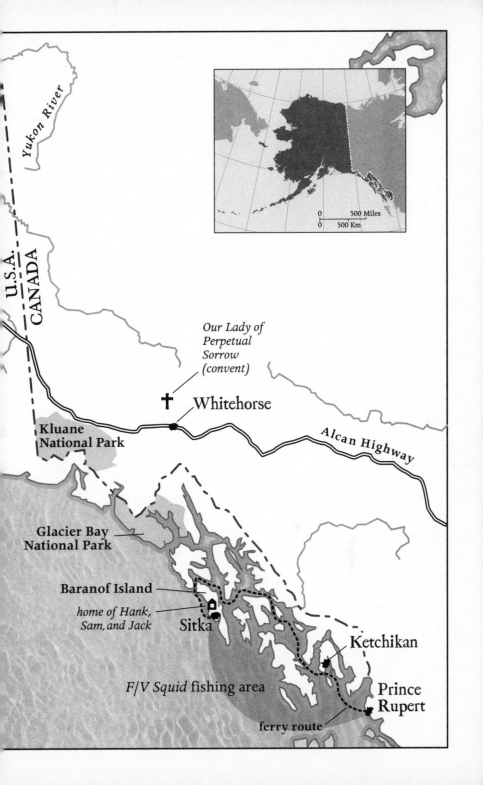

PROLOGUE

The Way Things Were Back Then

RUTH, 1958–63

I can't stop remembering the way things were *back then*. How my father hunted for our food. How he'd hang the deer in the garage to cure and how the deer's legs would splay out when its belly was sliced open, its hooves pointy like a ballerina's toes. I watched him dozens of times as he cut the meat off the animal's backside. I can still hear how the knife sounded when metal scraped bone. Backstrap was the best cut, my favorite, and Daddy sliced it off the deer's spine as beautifully as Mama curled ribbons on presents. He carried the fresh meat to the house in his bare hands, blood dripping all the way from the garage and across Mama's shiny linoleum to the kitchen sink.

Sometimes Daddy would bring me a still-warm deer heart

1

in a bowl and let me touch it with my fingers. I would put my lips to it and kiss its smooth, pink flesh, hoping to feel it beating, but it was all beat out. Mama would call him Daniel Boone as she laughed into his bare neck and he twirled his bloody fingers through her hair and they danced around the kitchen. Mama was the kind of person who put wildflowers in whiskey bottles. Lupine and foxglove in the kitchen, lilacs in the bathroom. She smelled like marshy muskeg after a hard rain, and even with blood in her hair, she was beautiful.

My easel was set up on the counter, so I could watch Mama cook the meat while I painted in the tutu Daddy had brought me from one of his many trips Outside. It had matching pink ballet slippers that I wore constantly, even to bed. Mama buttoned one of Daddy's big flannel shirts over me so I wouldn't ruin my special tutu. It hung all the way down to my toes; the long sleeves were rolled up so many times, it was like having big, bulging cinnamon rolls for arms. I tried to make red that was the same color as the red in Mama's hair, but mostly I mixed everything together and got brown.

Daddy often said things I didn't understand, like if statehood passed we would probably lose all of our hunting rights and the Feds would run everything into the ground. My five-year-old brain thought statehood was a new car, one with a really big front end. I didn't know who the Feds were, but Daddy seemed to think they were going to tell people how much venison and salmon they would be allowed to eat. Mama's belly had grown big and round, which even I knew meant another mouth to feed. Daddy would pull up her shirt and kiss her ballooned stomach the same way I had kissed the deer heart.

"Is it all beat out?" I asked him. Her belly was as white as the underside of a doe.

"This one's definitely still beating," he said. "No worries there."

Statehood turned out to be not a new car but something much, much bigger, and Daddy had to fly to Washington, DC, to try and stop it—a place where he had to show his passport just to get off the plane, and nobody hunted or fished, and he had to buy new shoes to go to a meeting to talk about why Alaskans didn't want statehood. Except for the ones who did, and they were not my daddy's friends.

He told me that most people didn't pay that much attention to stuff that happened in Washington, DC, but Alaskans would be sorry when Outside people started making decisions for us. I didn't know who these Outside people were, but I hoped I would never, ever meet them.

When the letter arrived in an envelope stamped with a flag I'd never seen before, Mama read it with shaking hands. I watched her lips moving without any sound, but I knew whatever it said was bad because she fell over clutching her belly, making sounds that I'd only heard from wild animals, deep in the woods.

Lily was born the day after the letter arrived, and I don't think Mama ever really saw her at all, because when I looked at Mama's eyes after the birth, they were blank.

The nurse asked what the baby's name would be, and when Mama said "Lily" I thought she was staring at the flowers next to her bed, not the pink lump wrapped in a hospital blanket, screaming as if she didn't want to be here, either. Gran had come to the hospital for the birth, but afterward Mama stayed behind while Lily and I were put in a moldy brown car with cigarette burns on the seats. I didn't think a brand-new baby should breathe in all the smells in that car, but Lily just lay there like the lump she was, and I held my scarf over my nose all the way to Gran's house in Birch Park.

"Your mama needs more time," Gran said, and she told me what was in the letter. My father's plane had crashed in the Canadian Arctic, right next door to Alaska. Gran said the men were on their way home from the meeting when the plane went down. Something about the way Gran talked told me she did not think Daddy was "a brave man, with big ideas for Alaska," which was what the letter had said. When Gran read it, she snorted, then wiped her nose with a tissue.

Afterward she said, "You can cry if you want, but it won't bring him back."

Birch Park smelled like an old person's house, something I'd never noticed when we only visited, which hadn't been very often. There were no flowers in whiskey bottles, no fresh deer carcasses curing from the rafters. The only meat in the refrigerator was pale and pink, sitting limp on a foam tray and wrapped in plastic. The blood was completely drained out of it, which made me homesick and suspicious.

The very next day there was a headline on the front page of the newspaper in thick, four-inch letters that said "We're In" and Alaska became the forty-ninth state in the United States. Gran clipped it out and told me I should save it forever so I would always remember this day, as if she didn't understand that this was a bad thing. I didn't want to remember anything except the way it used to be, before all this statehood nonsense.

When Mama did not show up that day, or the one after that or the one after that, I figured statehood must have done something to her, too. Maybe she didn't have the right passport or she had the wrong shoes? Or maybe she had gone to Canada, where she would be swallowed up in the same vast emptiness that had swallowed up Daddy.

I waited and waited for Mama, worried that Lily would never know how the world was really supposed to be. But the years ticked by until just before my tenth birthday, when the water started to rise and I knew this must be it— the river was fighting back. It flooded its banks and rose higher and higher, grabbing everything in sight with its big, wet tongue. Daddy had been right when he'd said the rivers could never be tamed.

Rusty metal oil drums, blue plastic coolers, and whole cans of peaches and fruit cocktail from people's pantries bobbed down Second Avenue. Someone's red frilly slip got hung up in Mr. Peterson's climbing peas and made Lily laugh out loud until Gran shushed her. Gran's face was as red as an overripe raspberry. Even in a flood, underwear was no joking matter.

Lily was now five and out of her mind with excitement

about riding in the skiff that snatched us off the doorstep as the water kept rising. I just prayed that it would never stop, that the river would somehow take us back to our old life.

But the skiffs dropped us off at the high school just a mile beyond our doorstep, where the ground was higher and still dry. Lily acted like we were on a whirlwind vacation, laughing and playing with her friend Bunny.

A girl named Selma held my hand when we had to get shots, and I acted like I was only clutching her hand to make her feel better, but really I'm terrified of needles. She was my age, but so much braver than me. Selma was the only good thing to come out of the flood.

After a few days we went home to the wet, moldy house in Birch Park. There was no furniture, just donated goods that had been trucked up from Anchorage. Under our used sneakers the carpet squelched and burped muddy water for weeks. Gran worked as a volunteer to get the new state government to replace what everyone had lost in the flood. Some of the neighbors reported a lot of missing items. Dora Peters's mom said she'd lost a washer and dryer, a kitchen table, and some fancy bedside lamps. Gran's lips were pursed, but she wrote it all down anyway in a big black book with "Property of the United States Government" printed on the front.

"Nobody in Birch Park had a washer or dryer," I said to Gran that night at dinner.

Gran said nothing.

"Can we get a washer and dryer?" asked Lily.

"Don't be silly," Gran snapped.

"But they lied," I said. "Nobody had all that nice stuff."

"It's not our job to make people accountable."

"But you're volunteering for the government. It is your job."

Gran's eyes narrowed.

"You do not tell me what is and isn't my job, young lady."

I looked down at the paper plate in my lap. The canned beets had bled into the Spam, which wasn't even real meat. I wanted a dripping piece of fresh backstrap or nothing. I folded my plate in two, smashing all the food together. No one said a word as I crossed the room, even as a trail of bloody beet juice spilled from the corner of the plate, down my leg, and onto the floor. I pushed the whole thing deep into the garbage can, as if it were my own heart, all beat out.

SPRING

So many spring stars
I could navigate my skiff
All the way back home.

—JOHN STRALEY

CHAPTER ONE

The Smell of
Other People's Houses

RUTH

At some point I stopped waiting for Mama to come back. It's hard to hold on to a five-year-old dream, and even harder to remember people after ten years. But I never stopped believing there had to be something better than Birch Park, something better than living with Gran.

When I was sixteen I thought maybe it was a boy named Ray Stevens. His father was a private detective and a hunting guide in the bush. His family had just built a new house on a lake where they parked their floatplane, and in winter they could snow-machine all the way down Moose Creek from their back door.

The Stevenses' whole house was made of fresh-cut cedar. All of Ray's clothes smelled like cedar, and it made me sneeze when I got close to him, but I got close anyway.

Cedar is the smell of swim team parties at their house and the big eight-by-ten-inch Richard Nixon photograph that hung in the living room. Cedar is the smell of Republicans. It's the smell of sneaking from Ray's older sister's room (Anna also swam on my relay team; I befriended her out of necessity) and into Ray's room, where I crawled into his queen-sized bed facing the sliding glass doors that looked out on the lake. How many sixteen-year-old boys had a queen-sized bed? I'm guessing one, and it had sheets that smelled like cedar and Tide, and they held a boy with curly blond hair, bleached from the swimming pool. He was the best diver in the state and I was only on a dumb relay team, but he sought me out anyway. We could have drowned in our combined smells of chlorine and ignorance—guess which part I was?

He knew how to French-kiss, which tasted like a forest of promises once I got used to it. Because I was Catholic, and smelled stiff instead of wild, he promised not to do anything but touch me lightly and only in certain places, where the smell wouldn't give me away when I went back to my own house, which held nothing but the faint scent of mold in secondhand furniture—also known as guilt and sin.

At the Stevenses', everything was fresh, like it had just been flown in from Outside, and there were no rules. Their shag carpet was so thick that in the morning I followed my deep orange footprints back to Ray's sister's room and pretended I'd been there all night.

*　*　*

I only joined the swim team because ballet hadn't worked out. Gran was sure that any kind of dancing was just a slippery slope that butted right up to the gates of vanity. In her opinion, there was nothing worse than being vain. Lily and I paid for our vanity little by little. We paid by hiding good report cards, deflecting compliments, and staying out of sight. We paid in the confessional on Sundays. *"Forgive me, Father, for I have sinned. I smiled at myself in the mirror today."*

I did that. Once. Felt so good about myself that I smiled into a mirror and twirled and danced as if I held the world in my six-year-old hands. I was going to my first dance class in my fancy pink tutu and my long blond hair was all the way down to my butt. It really was so thick and long that it made this cool scritchy-scratchy noise across the mesh fabric of my tutu when I swung my head from side to side. It was the tutu Daddy had bought me Outside. You couldn't get a tutu like this in Fairbanks, and I don't think Gran knew that it was special, or she never would have let me have something the other girls didn't. I was so excited, and as I came up to the studio, I remember another girl and her mom going inside, too. Alyce was wearing a black leotard and plain pink tights. I could tell she was jealous, eyeing my tutu as she held open the door to let me in, and her mother said, "You have the prettiest long hair I've ever seen."

"I know. I'm pretty all over," I said to her without a second thought.

Alyce's mother smiled at me, but then her face changed

quickly as Gran's fingers gripped me by the arm and yanked me inside. I didn't even have time to wonder what I'd said that was wrong. Gran marched me into the bathroom, and said through gritted teeth, "Oh, you think you're something special, do you?"

She pulled a huge pair of orange-handled scissors out of her bag, as if she carried them around waiting for moments just like this. They looked like a bird with a silver metal beak. And they were *loud*. I can still hear the sound of my hair being chopped off with just a few mad snaps of the bird's jaws. Then Gran made me walk out of the bathroom and go take my place on the piece of tape that Miss Judy put on the floor marking my spot. Nobody looked right at me, but there were mirrors on every wall, so I could see their sideways glances. I could also see my hair sticking out in all directions, as if it had been caught in a lawn mower. No more swishing for me. I never went back to that class. And Gran never mentioned it again.

Even after all these years, I know that a stroke of good luck, like a rich, popular boyfriend whose family likes you, means you just have to hold your breath and hope it lasts— and never, ever brag or feel too good about yourself.

That's why I stole one of Ray's white T-shirts and took it home to sleep with under my pillow so I could pretend my world smelled of cedar, too. No one ever suspected anything, because at Birch Park, where the sound of cockroaches chewing saltines is deafening, I just kept my head down and let Lily make all the mistakes.

"Bunny says we're poor," Lily announces as she and her best friend, Bunny, clatter through the door, letting in a gust of cold air. They drop their mittens and snowsuits into a big pile and trip out of their boots, knocking each other over trying not to be late for dinner.

Gran is reheating food left over after another Catholic Social Services luncheon. She works part-time typing for the archbishop, so we get first dibs on whatever food is left from their functions. Tonight's meal was delivered to the door by Father Mike himself, with his little white collar choking him.

Selma is over and we're setting the table. I can see Gran looking at the food, wondering if it will be enough to feed two extra mouths. She reaches for a can of Spam to stretch it out.

"I didn't say you were poor. I said you were poorer than me and Dumpling," Bunny says. Dumpling is her older sister.

I watch Gran sigh, which is a sign that we're aging her. We're always aging her, but especially Lily, and now Bunny is helping. Gran says if she didn't have to take care of us, she'd still be a young woman. I look at her sagging boobs, then down at the tuna casserole. Too bad for Lily, there are peas in it again.

"What makes you so rich?" she asks Bunny as they jostle each other at the sink, fighting over the Joy soap.

"Fish camp," says Bunny, "We get tons and tons of salmon at fish camp."

"My cousin goes fishing every summer," Selma chimes in. "She doesn't think salmon are so special. In fact, Lily, I'm sure Alyce would trade places with you—she would *love* not to have fish this summer."

Selma's cousin Alyce is the same Alyce from that fateful ballet class. It was her mother who told me my hair was pretty.

"I don't want to go *commercial* fishing and have to live on a smelly old boat," Lily says, as if she's just been insulted. "I want to go to fish camp like Bunny and Dumpling, near their village."

"Yeah," Bunny says, "our camp is way up above the Arctic Circle. We have drumming circles and dances that go on all night, and then we lay our sleeping bags out on spruce boughs and we don't have to get up until the afternoon if we don't want to. Me and Dumpling get to shoot mice with BB guns and roast salmon hearts over the fire, too. Better than marshmallows!" She rubs her belly and licks her lips just thinking about it.

I'll pass on the roasted salmon hearts. But Bunny sounds braggy to me, and I glance over at Gran to see if she's ruffled by it. She's spooning food onto plates as if it takes so much concentration. I guess other people's kids can be vain if they want. Lily better watch out it doesn't rub off on her.

"Is there mayonnaise in this?" Lily asks.

She is the pickiest eater on the planet.

"Lily," Gran says in a voice that lets Lily know mayonnaise should be the least of her worries. "Say grace."

"Blessusolordandtheseourgiftswhichweareabouttoreceive fromthybountythroughchristourlordamenwhy-can't-we-have-a-fish-camp?" Lily asks, without taking a breath.

Selma looks at me and we roll our eyes. Lily spends her life griping that almost everyone else in Birch Park has a fish camp. But saying it in front of Bunny puts Gran on the spot. It also shows how clueless both Lily and Bunny are if they haven't figured this one out yet. They're both eleven, which is plenty old enough know to where the lines are drawn.

"We don't have a fish camp because we aren't native," Gran says, to her plate.

"I'm not native, I'm Athabascan," Bunny says.

Selma and I laugh.

"What's so funny? She is Athabascan," says Lily. "Natives are the people like Dora's mom, the ones who hang out all day at the bar—they're too drunk to even bother fishing."

"That's enough," Gran says, slapping Lily so hard on the hand that her fork flies up and then falls with a clatter.

"No more talking while we eat this meal that Father Mike has so generously provided for us."

Lily pushes her peas around on her plate. Her cheeks are bright pink.

Fish camps are pretty much handed down from family to family, but maybe Gran shouldn't have lumped all Alaska Natives together. It didn't seem to make Bunny very happy. Especially because Bunny and Dumpling actually have the nicest parents in Birch Park. Dora's family never goes to fish camp. Lily knows better than to gossip about Dora at the table, though.

It's not as if we all didn't see what happened the night Dora came running out of her house wearing only a nightgown. Her father, Bumpo, was chasing after her, calling her a whore. I think he got the name Bumpo because he's always drunk and bumping into things. Bunny's dad, Mr. Moses, was the only person brave enough to go outside and face him. Mr. Moses had a big wool blanket and he scooped Dora up in it like she was just a sack of feathers; then he set her inside the door of his own house. No matter how much Bumpo yelled in his face or threatened him with a beer bottle, Mr. Moses didn't budge; he just stood there blocking the door that hid Dora.

It went on and on until Bumpo just sort of slumped over, all deflated. Bunny's father led Bumpo back to his house. And the rest of us went back to pretending we didn't see anything.

If you're wondering why nobody called the cops, that would show how little you know about us. Whatever you happen to be—black, white, native, or purple, it doesn't matter—it's a sin to snitch. It's the one universal rule that being poor will buy you, for better or worse.

When Gran gets up from the table and is out of earshot, good old Selma leans in to Lily and says, "I thought the Lord provided the meal, not Father Mike." All she gets is a half-hearted smile from my sister, who is busy piling her peas onto Bunny's plate now that Gran isn't looking.

Bunny eats them all in one bite, because that's what best friends do. Then they both hop up saying they're going to Bunny's for Eskimo ice cream and are out the door before Gran can argue.

Lily has Bunny and I have Selma. And that's why we haven't gone totally batshit crazy yet, living with Gran.

Selma is the complete opposite of me. She came into the world in the most unconventional way and must have decided before she was even three days old that she was going to fall in love with her life, no matter what. (It helps that she doesn't live with someone who might chop off her hair.) Selma has these enormous brown eyes like a seal, and for whatever reason, she doesn't feel bound by the same rules as the rest of us, which makes her a great friend. But she doesn't live in Birch Park, and I'm reminded of that when I hear a timid knock at the door, so light that Gran doesn't hear it in the kitchen.

Selma's wide eyes are laughing around the edges as she mouths silently, "Alyce."

Alyce will sometimes drop by and pick Selma up on her way home from ballet. They both live on the other side of the river, where the houses get nicer in a hurry and the rent is much higher.

Alyce is long and lean with high cheekbones. Her hair is pinned perfectly into a bun. She's wearing leg warmers, too, which might be fine at ballet, but in Birch Park I'm sure anyone who sees her just thinks she cut the sleeves off her sweater and is wearing them on her legs. She always looks terrified when she comes to pick up Selma. I'm not sure what she thinks will happen to her here; all she's doing is standing on our doorstep.

"Ready to go?" she says to Selma, barely acknowledging me.

The only reason she steps inside is because it's twenty below on the porch.

"Hi, Alyce," I say.

"Hi," she mumbles, looking down at the puddles of melting snow from her boots. "Too bad you missed Lily," Selma says, as if Alyce cares. "She'd love to talk to you about fishing. Maybe you could convince your dad to take her on as a deckhand and you could get a summer off?"

"Selma—" Alyce looks embarrassed.

"There's a recruiter coming from one of the top dance colleges this summer," Selma says to me, "but Alyce can't get out of fishing with her dad, so she doesn't get to audition."

"Selma," Alyce says, "your mom's going to be worried. You know how she is; we should go."

Selma is pulling on her snow pants, completely unfazed and unaware that Alyce is so uncomfortable. I run my fingers through my hair and then stop when Alyce glances my way. She has tiny startled eyes like a baby bird, and when she looks at me I know exactly what she is thinking. Neither of us will ever forget Gran chopping off my hair.

Boo-hoo, no college scout for Alyce, I think as she looks quickly back down at the floor. At least Alyce has the decency to be embarrassed. But not Selma.

"I don't see why you don't just ask your dad," she says, struggling into her parka. "Or get your mom to tell him. How hard can that be?"

Alyce's bun is starting to come undone from its bobby pins, as if Selma's talking about her is making it unravel bit by bit. I'm tempted to reach out and spin her like a top. Would she unspool all the way down to her bright-pink leg warmers?

"Her parents don't really get along," Selma says, now rummaging through the milk crate where we keep hats and old woolen socks that we wear in layers on our hands. Cheaper than buying mittens.

"Yours are on top," I tell her, pointing to the pair that Selma knit herself, as if anyone could miss them. The thumbs are twice the size they should be and they are fluorescent orange.

As much as I like Selma, in certain situations she can be kind of oblivious. Suddenly I'm as anxious to get Alyce out of our doorway as Alyce is to leave.

"Thanks for dinner," Selma yells at Gran as they open the door; Alyce practically leaps into the snowbank trying to get away. Even in a panicked rush, she is the most graceful person I've ever seen, and I cannot picture her working on a stinky boat gutting fish, no matter how hard I try. Selma smiles and waves good-bye, then links her arm with Alyce's and I watch their shadows bob away under the yellow street-lights. How does Selma manage to break all the rules and still stay on everyone's good side?

But maybe it's my turn to break some rules, too, because don't forget, I have a rich boyfriend who flicked me on the butt one day with his wet towel at swim practice and said, "Want to come to a party at my house after the meet?"

After I stayed over that first time, all I wanted was to stay over again. But Gran only lets us go to a friend's house once a month. Until next month, I have to settle for calling Ray late at night, from the phone in the hallway.

The long red cord stretches into my room, where I put his shirt over my head and listen to his voice telling me about the northern lights outside his window, streaking across the sky and then bouncing off the frozen lake in big, fat, wavy swaths of green and red and yellow.

We talk about swim practice and I lick chlorine off my arm, pretending it's his. He tells me where I should touch myself and promises all kinds of things for the next time I sleep over. I ask him why his family likes Richard Nixon so much and he says he doesn't know, but that his dad some-times calls him "Tricky Dicky." He says he wants to come to Birch Park sometime, but I hope he's just saying that to be nice. I would die if he saw where I live.

"Your house smells so much better than mine," I tell him.

I've realized over time that houses with moms in them do tend to smell better. If I close my eyes, I can just barely remember my mother's wildflowers in their whiskey bottles. The very distant scent of my parents lingers in my brain, as they laugh and twirl around the kitchen. Deer blood on my father's hands tinges all my memories of them—their skin, their hair, their clothes. The smell of too much love.

I don't say any of this to Ray, who still has two parents and a house that smells like store-bought everything. I don't want to scare him away.

Finally I get to stay over again, and this time Ray has a little foil packet the size of a tea bag that he says we should use, just to be safe. But every Catholic knows that's the worst sin of all. After asking me about six times if I'm sure I don't want to use it, he gives up and we get drunk on each other, practically drowning in a blur of skin and hair and tangled sheets. I don't even think about how this part is probably a sin, too. Ray keeps calling me "beautiful" over and over and over, until I even start believing him. It's as if someone is seeing me for the first time in my life.

I fall asleep right there next to him, totally naked, and forget to go back to Anna's room. Suddenly Mrs. Stevens walks in with a pile of freshly folded shirts. It's morning; the sun is streaming in through the big glass windows and I have never been more embarrassed.

"Oh, sorry," she says when she sees us, "didn't mean to barge in." As she backs out the door, her cloudy blue eyes look sad and weirdly guilty, as if she's the one who's been caught.

"Oh my God. Isn't she mad?" I ask Ray, pulling the sheet over my head. If that had been Gran, they'd be ordering my coffin.

But Ray just laughs and tries to roll on top of me.

"What can she say? It's not like Anna isn't here because my mom did the same thing back in high school. Why do you think she had to get married so young?"

He reaches out to touch my breast but I push his hand away, struggling to get back into my nightgown. I feel queasy and can't stop seeing his mother's blue, blue eyes, as if they are the sea and I have just swum way too far from shore.

CHAPTER TWO

The Ice Classic

DORA

Crazy Dancing Guy is on the corner and we pretend not to see him, which is sort of impossible. He's always in that big fluffy hat with the pom-pom; an insulated Carhartt suit; and white, clomping bunny boots dancing away like he's in his own kitchen, radio blaring. He does disco-pointing, hip-swinging, foot-stomping, jumping-around-looking-weird dance moves on this corner every single day. How could we not see him? He is out here even when it's forty below. But at forty below, at least dancing around makes sense.

Everyone who lives in Birch Park has to walk by him when we leave school, which is the one equalizer among us, besides also having to find a way to stay warm. Being poor may be enough to make us all look like a bunch of mismatched, unfashionable orphans, but it isn't enough to make us all friends.

Ruth Lawrence and her friend Selma Flowers are walking ahead of me and Dumpling. Selma doesn't even live in Birch Park, but she walks home with Ruth every day because her mom is a fancy-pants reporter at the paper and the over-protective type, which means Selma can't be home alone, even at the age of sixteen. Selma's adopted, which would be no big deal, except that she loves talking about it.

You can tell she is not from a village. In a village, it doesn't matter who belongs to who. There are so many kids, they just bounce from house to house. If you happen to notice that your auntie's new baby doesn't look anything like her husband—but more like one of the guys from upriver who comes down in the spring to fish—you just smile and pinch his chubby cheeks anyway, because who cares? It's not Selma's life that makes her different from us, it's the fact that she talks about it.

She and Ruth both wear hand-knitted scarves and bulky hats that keep falling over their eyes. There must have been a big sale on orange yarn. Every day it seems like they have one more newly knitted item that doesn't fit. One of them is suddenly into arts and crafts.

Dumpling thinks Ruth is all right—maybe it's just because she's Lily's sister and everyone loves Lily. But if the rumor about Ruth and Ray Stevens is true, she's definitely not very smart.

He sat behind me in social studies all last year and kept

saying things like "Does anyone else smell muktuk?" Oh, that's original. Of course all of us smell like whale blubber. It's such an old racist joke I can't even give him points for trying. No matter how much I ignored him he didn't let up. I've never told anyone, not even Dumpling, about the note he slid onto my desk when nobody was looking. It said, "I could do things to you with my oosik that would make your fat bubble-gum ass dance." I had nightmares for a week about that, even though he spelled it wrong. The word for whale penis is *usruk*, smart-ass. How could Dumpling think Ruth is okay if she likes someone like that?

But Dumpling always takes the high road. I'm sure she and her sister, Bunny, are nice because they have such nice parents, but as a matter of survival, I don't take people at face value. I wait. Some people may look harmless, but most are just waiting to flare up and burn you if you get too close. You can never be too careful.

Dumpling's dad taught her that the glass is half full; mine taught me that the glass is totally full—of whiskey. Not very many people have a father like Dumpling's, which is too bad for the rest of us. Sometimes I pretend, just for a few minutes every night before I go to sleep, that her dad is actually my dad, too, and that's the only time I get any sleep.

Most people in Fairbanks just lump all native people together, like the lunch lady who asked if Dumpling and I were sisters. I wish. Never mind that our Athabascan and Inupiat ancestors fought each other—she's Indian; I'm Eskimo. Nobody would ever confuse Lily and Bunny like that—except maybe Lily and Bunny, who are walking in front of us now in their hand-me-down snowsuits, arms linked together, their heads practically touching, talking nonstop as they trudge between mounds of dirty snow. One dishwater blond like a hawk, the other jet-black like a raven. As usual, they're laughing their heads off about something, probably that dumb Liquid Drano commercial they're always reciting. The rest of us remember coming to Birch Park, but Bunny and Lily were too young. They've been inseparable since the moment they first laid eyes on each other.

As I get up to the corner, Crazy Dancing Guy yells to me, "What didn't you fail at today?" Then he lists off a stream of numbers like he's a drill sergeant. "Eighteen, seven, three, forty-two, nine."

I ignore him. He always yells the same thing and then random numbers. Nobody knows what he's talking about. But as I turn the corner on Second Avenue, his words curl around my head like ice fog. I failed at everything today. I failed at getting to school on time and turning in my algebra paper. I failed at keeping the nightmares at bay and not sleeping with a chair propped under the doorknob, even though nothing has happened in months and I sleep at Dumpling's now. I failed at telling myself I would not let Crazy Dancing Guy make me count off on my fingers all the ways I failed at not failing.

Later, Mom comes over to Dumpling's and says she'll drive me to the Salvation Army to look for some new snow boots. I need to say that again: *Mom says she'll drive me to the Salvation Army to look for some new snow boots.* That seems like such a small, ordinary thing, but remember I live with Dumpling now. Her father brings home moose and caribou and ptarmigan, and her mother cooks them up on top of their woodstove in these huge cast-iron pots and the whole house smells like it's smothered in gravy. Nobody yells at each other and throws pictures that will break in their frames and then get hung right back up on the wall anyway. At Dumpling's you don't have to look through shattered glass to see whose face it is, looking back out, warning you that the sound of glass breaking means it's time to hide.

So when Mom comes over to Dumpling's house like she's just a friendly neighbor offering to take me to the Salvation Army, I wonder what's up. I know Dumpling's father does, too, but nobody is going to say anything because that's not what we do. Dumpling's father shrugs and fiddles with his suspenders while her mother spoons Crisco into an empty coffee can and nods at the frozen blueberries in the sink, reminding me that the akutuq, Eskimo ice cream, will be ready when I get back.

"She makes that just for you?" Mom asks as we climb into her rusty blue Chevy. I shrug and make sure to hook the bungee cord really tight. It keeps the door from swinging open on the corners. Another thing I like about being at Dumpling's is that her mother knows my favorite dessert and goes out of her way to make it for me without drawing a lot of attention to it. Also, there are real locks on all the doors.

I don't say anything, and my voice would be drowned out by the sound of the Chevy's muffler even if I did. Bunny and Lily are on the merry-go-round, spinning and laughing. They yell something in unison, and even though I can't hear, I imagine it's another commercial.

As we drive away, I watch them spinning faster and faster on the merry-go-round, another gift from Catholic Charities for the poor kids of Birch Park, their arms draped over each other's shoulders as if they are the only two people in a world they have created just for themselves. How do they do that?

At the corner of Bartlett and Second Avenue, Crazy Dancing Guy is still doing his thing.

Mom honks and smiles. "I love him."

"Mom, don't encourage him. He looks stupid."

"He makes people laugh. He makes people feel good."

"He's pickled," I say before I can stop myself, and she slaps me with the back of her hand, right across my cheek. So fast I never even saw it coming.

"You know better," she says, lighting up her cigarette, tossing the match out the window. "You starting to think you're better than us now, 'cause you live with rich people and eat akutuq every day?"

I ignore that she thinks eating lard mixed with sugar and berries somehow makes you rich. But it's really her way of saying she sees what Dumpling's mother does for me. If I didn't know her better, I might think it bothers her, but that would mean she cares and I don't let myself go there. Not after all the times she just stood by and did nothing.

I silently tick off three more things I have failed at today. Understanding my mom, remembering that we never talk about other people's problems (or our own), and convincing Mom not to honk and wave at Crazy Dancing Guy.

"Is he native?" I ask her, trying to make it sound like I didn't just accuse someone's parents of drinking so much that their kid came out fermented and weird, and now dances on a street corner. He doesn't really look native, but that doesn't mean he's not. There's a bunch of kids down in Caribou Flats who have bright-red hair, because they have an Athabascan mom and a Scottish dad. Now, there's a family who knows how to laugh and drink and break a lot of furniture.

"Nobody knows," she says, also happy to turn the talk back to Crazy Dancing Guy. "I heard he calls himself 'Miscellaneous.'"

"That's just weird," I say, rubbing my cheek.

"Come on, Dora, he's *funny*. He brightens up the day when it's so dark and cold out."

"He's mental, Mom." Unlike "pickled," my mother seems to think "mental" is a compliment.

"Some of my favorite people are mental." She laughs and takes a drag on her cigarette. My mom loves to laugh,

31

especially when nothing is funny. It's an important trait to have around here, but I'm afraid I didn't inherit it.

At the Salvation Army, we run into my mom's friends, Paula and Annette, the loud sisters. I go to the shoe section by myself, but I can hear Mom howling with them a few aisles away, probably in the old lady pants section. The whole place smells like everyone's mudroom in spring during break-up season, moldy and sweaty with a hint of thawing dog shit, because it's on the bottom of every shoe.

There are lots of big white bunny boots here, but I do not want to look like Crazy Dancing Guy, even though they are the smartest choice and the cheapest. But then I spot them: Lobbens, woolen boots from Norway that the rich white girls wear. They look like elf shoes, but I know they're expensive and warm. Even at the Salvation Army these are ten bucks. I put them on and feel my feet slide around a bit, but with a few more pairs of socks they might work. I steer my Lobbened feet toward what sounds like moose braying, and sure enough, when Paula and Annette see me they practically pee their pants.

"The Keebler elves called, girl. They want their boots back!" Annette falls on top of Paula, who is wearing a red and white sweater covered in snowmen and a pair of reindeer antlers. All the Christmas stuff is seventy-five percent off right now.

I ignore Annette. "Mom, can I get these?"

My mom clutches her stomach like she's trying to keep her spleen from bursting.

"They're warm and a little big, so they'll last a long time."

"Go ask George if I got any more credit," she says, draping her arm around Paula for balance and knocking off her antlers. "If they're so warm maybe you can walk yourself home. Oh, and tell George I need the change; we're going to stop off at the Sno-Go for happy hour."

So there it is, the reason my mom offered to bring me here for boots. She didn't have any cash for the bar.

George winks at me out of a face that looks like a baked apple with tiny cloves for eyes. He knew my great-grandparents back in the village, he's that old.

"You okay, Dora? Those don't look like your usual style."

"I like these, George. They're really warm."

"I know, those European dog mushers have been wearing them lately in all the races. But I didn't think you were the dog mushing type."

"No, I just like them. A change, you know?"

"Does your mama know they're ten dollars?"

I shrug. Surely she was hoping George would give her at least seven bucks back. The Salvation Army is kind of like a neighborhood bank. You get credit for bringing in old clothes, but then if you buy at least five dollars' worth of merchandise, you can take the rest of your balance in change.

"Well, would you look at that," he says, punching a few keys on his register. "Foreign merchandise is on sale today and today only. It's your lucky day, Dora." He winks and hands me eight bucks.

What I like about George is this: He lets people make their own choices. He doesn't judge anyone or try to talk me out of something that is a very bad idea. And when I come back two days later with my old sneakers on because I would rather freeze than endure another day of the rich girls at school laughing and pointing and saying I'm trying to be like them, George does not say, "No, you can't return these European, snobby woolen boots and trade them for the bunny boots you should have bought to begin with."

All he says is "You'll get a five-dollar credit on that exchange, if you want to grab some socks or something nice for yourself." I don't tell George that this is the Salvation Army, so finding something nice for myself is probably a long shot. Besides, my mother would absolutely know if I got cash credit and didn't give it to her.

When I walk back past Second Avenue in the bunny boots, all Crazy Dancing Guy says to me is, "What didn't you fail at today? Five, four, ten, thirty-seven." He does not stop dancing. Arms and legs flying, cars honking, him smiling and waving. He says it twice more, "Five, four, ten, thirty-seven," so that the numbers stick in my head like a song. Just when I think he's done he yells, "I like your boots."

Dumpling runs up from behind and links my arm with hers, completely ignoring Crazy Dancing Guy.

"Hey, Dora."

"Hey, Dumpling."

She swings her braid around and smacks me in the face with the red ribbon that she wears every single day.

"Where you off to?" she asks, looking at my boots and of course not mentioning it.

I flash the five-dollar bill in my mittened hand and she knows that I'm on my way to the Sno-Go to give my mother her change.

"Bunny was named for those boots," she says.

"What were you named for?" I ask.

"Some dish one of the priests made for my mom when she was pregnant with me, chicken and dumplings? It's the only time my mom had chicken. She said it's just like ptarmigan, but not as tender."

We laugh at the utter practicality of Dumpling's parents, which makes me feel all warm inside until I get a whiff of something dark and smoky, like burnt toast, which I recognize as the smell of my family compared to hers. I wonder if a person can ever really shake where they come from.

"Want me to come with you to the Sno-Go?" she asks.

"Oh, you don't have to. I know you can't stand all the smoke."

She turns and presses her face close to mine.

"Please don't make me go home. Bunny and Lily are driving me mad with the TV. They don't even watch the shows; they just wait for the commercials and then turn the volume up to about a million."

It's just like Dumpling to act like I'm doing her a favor by letting her come with me to the bar. "All right, if it means so much to you," I say. The truth is, I kind of have a soft spot for the Sno-Go, because it was there that my father lost his temper and shot up the bathroom with a rifle. And that's why he got thrown into the slammer. He didn't hurt anyone; he just went in there drunk and decided to remodel the bathroom with a gun. So now he's in jail for "reckless endangerment" and I can sleep at night—more or less—as long as I'm at Dumpling's and her dad makes sure to bolt the front door.

It's only four p.m. but the Sno-Go is packed. I secretly love the way the cigarette smoke billows out the door and mixes with the ice fog. When we step inside, nobody knows who we are for half a second while the air settles. Then they all see us. There's a few high-pitched whistles, lots of laughter. Dumpling's parents never come to the bar, but my mom is here every single day with her loud-sister pals.

"You got a credit from George," I tell Mom, once we make our way over to where she sits with Paula and Annette. "Can Dumpling and I have a couple dollars, though, for a Dairy Queen?" She grabs the bill from my hand with a big, dimpled grin and I know it's as good as spent.

But I made sure to ask within hearing distance of Paula. "Wait, it's on me, you two," she says right on cue, whipping out her beaded wallet. Paula can be very generous after a few drinks, which makes me think she's had an okay childhood.

I will never touch booze and I hope to God that's a promise I can say I didn't fail at.

"Thanks, Paula," I say as she gives me a wadded-up bunch of bills and a messy, pungent kiss on the cheek.

Nick is behind the bar and calls us over. My mom dated Nick for a while after Dad left. I liked him more than the others. Even though he tends bar, he never came home drunk. And he's got nice teeth, which you don't see every day.

"You girls wanna Ice Classic ticket? You could win thousands."

The Ice Classic has been going on for almost seventy years. For one buck per ticket, people guess when the ice on the river is going to go out, and if they're right, they win a load of cash. Last year it was something crazy, like ten thousand dollars. There's a tripod set up on the middle of the frozen river with a trip wire and a clock that stops at the exact time the ice goes out. The winner is the one closest right down to the minute. It's hard to think about the river thawing when it's still forty below. But when spring finally does come, it rushes in like a band of robbers. The gunshot sound of ice breaking frightens me every single year.

"Come on, ladies, one buck. Change your lives forever. Can't really go wrong with just one buck."

"That means no Dairy Queen," whispers Dumpling.

"No, it means no dipped cone. We can just get a plain swirl if we each use one buck here."

Dumpling is thinking hard about this. She loves cherry-dipped cones.

"I think it's a sure fail," she says. "I mean, come on, the exact minute?"

Crazy Dancing Guy's voice is still spinning around in my brain. Five, four, ten, thirty-seven . . .

"One ticket, Nick," I hear myself say. I take the stub and fill in the blank. May 4, 10:37 a.m.

We head back out into the cold, and if Dumpling is wondering what I just did, she doesn't ask. I'm not sure I even know myself.

"Hey, Dumpling, when Crazy Dancing Guy asks what you didn't fail at today, what do you think of?"

"Right now, I would say I didn't fail at getting a cherry-dipped cone, but you did."

SUMMER

Sun, Sun where do you live?
Where do you live in summer?
I live in my house at the top of the world,
At the top of the world in summer.

—NANCY WHITE CARLSTROM

CHAPTER THREE

Ballerina Fish Slayer

ALYCE

While I wait for my Dad to finish up some last-minute details back in town, I sit on the boat reading old copies of the police blotter in the local paper. It's better than the funnies. Like this one:

> *Salty Blotter, June 28, 1970: 12:15 p.m. Police received a report that a man was beating a child in the 200 block of Marine Way, but when officers arrived it appeared the two were just having a dandelion fight.*

The police blotter will tell you everything you never wanted to know about this place. Here's an example of the way nothing happens here and then becomes news:

June 29, 1970: 2:10 a.m. A woman reported three boys missing from their home on Klondike Alley. When police arrived to investigate, a man who answered the door said it was just a misunderstanding and the boys were asleep in their beds.

See what I mean? Boys asleep in their beds is hot news. This place is weird.

I was born in this tiny fishing town on the edge of the Pacific Ocean, but I don't really remember living here. Most of my life was spent on our boat, the *Squid,* until my parents divorced and Mom moved us to Fairbanks to be closer to her sister, Aunt Abigail. My cousin Selma was born here, too, but like me she doesn't remember it.

Aunt Abigail adopted her when she was only a few days old, and Selma doesn't know who her parents are. She loves imagining them, though, and sometimes it's tiring, listening to her fantasize about her real parents. Everything from her mother being half human/half seal living in the ocean, to her explorer father running an oil tanker back and forth from Russia to Alaska. None of it is true, but try telling Selma that.

"Hey, Alyce, can you retie the bow line? We're getting too far away from the dock and I need to unload this thing."

My uncle is coming down the dock with a cart full of groceries. Oops.

"Sorry, Uncle Gorky, I got sidetracked."

Groceries are my job.

"I can take it from here," I tell him, and he does that silent nod accompanied by a slight shrug that fishermen are known for; then he hops onto the boat.

Without another word he grabs a pair of insulated gloves and jumps down into the fish hold to start moving ice around. He calls it "making up the beds" for the salmon we're going to catch.

"We're the Holland America *Squid*," he likes to joke, a cruise ship for dead fish. Uncle Gorky does all the icing—tucking of the fish into their beds, as it were—to keep them cool until we can make it to the processors to sell them.

When I was two, I called them bald little babies. Apparently I used to kiss every single fish before it was put down to bed in the fish hold, or so the story goes.

Uncle Gorky didn't fish then, just me and my parents. I've been told that if my father tried to speed up the process and throw a couple down without me seeing, I would scream my head off until he climbed down and got them again so I could kiss them good night. One of a million stories, as it happens, that I hear from both my parents over and over again.

We used to live on the boat all year round until I was five. That's when Mom took us to the interior part of the state, where there's no sea—just mountains and tundra and long ribbons of rivers. I know she misses being near the ocean. Just the other day when we were at the airport waiting for my flight, she was dabbing her eyes and sniffling as she handed me my float coat.

"I just miss it," she said.

It, not *him.*

"Don't forget you have to pull the cord to inflate your coat," she told me as if I was still two.

"Mom, I know that. Duh."

My dance friends, Sally and Izzy, had come to the airport to say good-bye, and it was embarrassing that they had to hear Mom talk to me like that.

"Let's go get some gum in the gift shop," Izzy whispered.

"I just don't understand how she can still get so emotional after this many years," I told them.

But when I glanced back at her sitting at the gate holding my dry bag and rubber boots, I felt a twinge of guilt. She and Dad just couldn't make it work, so she gave up a life she loved and came here, where she had more "emotional support," as she says.

Sally and Izzy have never been out of Fairbanks, but they're both hoping to get college scholarships and go Outside to major in dance. The thing is, you have to audition the summer before senior year—*this* summer—because schools are looking way down the road. It's too late once you've graduated. We were supposed to be the *Swan Lake* version of the Three Musketeers, always together, even in college.

They're trying not to show it, but I can tell I'm letting them down by going fishing. I can't imagine either of them working on a boat, touching a slimy salmon, or even having to set a dainty foot on a blood-soaked deck.

"Did you ask if you could come back in a couple weeks,

just for the audition?" Izzy asked, holding up a sweatshirt showing a cartoon moose batting its eyes and wearing bright-red lipstick. It said, "I'll moose you when you leave Alaska." Tourists will buy anything.

"It's too expensive to fly back and forth. Besides, my dad needs me for the whole summer; it's a lot of work."

"Too bad your mom can't fill in for you," Sally said, looking over at Mom holding on to my float coat as if somehow she needed it to keep her head above water, even in the middle of a landlocked airport.

But Mom's never going fishing again and there's no way I can tell Dad that I don't want to go, either. Worse than not getting the audition would be getting accepted, which would mean attending preprofessional classes next summer before the official college courses start. I would never be able to skip a whole summer of fishing; it's the only time I see my dad.

Sally and Izzy mean well, but they have simple parents who are married and like to volunteer to sweep snow backstage at *The Nutcracker*. *The Nutcracker* is my winter life, where I get minor roles because everyone else has danced all summer and is in way better shape. My mom comes to it—she usually volunteers to sell tickets—but my dad has never seen me dance. Dad's life, and mine with him, is on the boat.

If I didn't fish, who would bag the salmon eggs and make sure the bloodlines along the coho backbones are totally clean? Those have been my jobs since forever. Dad says not even Uncle Gorky can cut the heads off as cleanly as I do, right through the neck bone. I don't explain that to Sally and Izzy. It's another world, another language.

When my flight was announced, we shuffled back to the gate where Mom had to make one last attempt to show my friends how smart she was about all things fish-related.

"Don't forget to pour a can of Coke in the washer to get the fish-blood smell out of your clothes," she said.

"Dad says you used to puke through the whole season. How can you miss it?" I asked.

"Perhaps your father should try fishing when he's six months pregnant."

Nice one, Mom.

Pregnant.

With me.

Everything is always my fault.

Sally and Izzy just stood there with fake smiles pasted on their faces, as if they were watching a dance choreographed by my mother and me where we alternate playing the tragic heroine depending on whose song is loudest. She loves fishing, but not my dad. I love my dad, but I'm tired of fishing. Especially when it gets between me and other things I love.

"Earth to Alyce," Dad says, swinging his legs over the side and climbing aboard. He caught me sitting on the fish hold, flexing the toes of my rubber boots, admiring my extension.

"Did you put the groceries away?" he asks.

"Of course; labeled all the cans, too."

Canned goods go under the floor in the galley, and my job is to write the contents on the top of each lid so you can read them by looking down from above. Apparently I learned to write by spelling *corned beef hash* and *kidney beans* on the tin lids. Every single thing on this boat is either about me or about how my parents lived their lives through me. "Do you want the big bunk?" Dad asks.

"Really? I can have it?"

It's a great bunk. Dad had wanted Mom to be happy, and being a man of very few words, he'd widened the bunk for his pregnant wife and thought that would be enough. Maybe it had worked for a little while anyway.

I fly down into the fo'c'sle and quickly claim the space before he changes his mind. I can hear my uncle moving totes around on deck, and without even seeing him I know there's a cigarette hanging from his lips and a steaming mug within his reach, no less than six Lipton tea bags in it. Uncle Gorky is a recovering alcoholic, so he has other vices to see him through a fishing trip.

Dad starts up the engine and the noise down here is deafening, although I know it won't take long to get used to and soon will sound no louder than a purring kitten. I breathe in diesel, the smell of my childhood, of sleeping in the belly of this boat that has always made my dreams bouncy. I never sleep as well anywhere as I do here on the *Squid*. And now I get the big bunk, too, which even has a little shelf built in for all my favorite books to make it cozier. See how hard my dad tried?

There's a nail sticking out of the wooden beam, and I remember the bouquet of dried wildflowers my mom had hung there, even though flowers are supposed to be bad luck on a boat. Maybe they were? I hang my pointe shoes on the nail and scramble up to help untie.

Dad is already talking on the VHF radio, which is the only time he actually seems to enjoy talking. The slow, drawling voice on the other end is obviously Dad's oldest fishing pal, *Sunshine* Sam. People are known by their boat name first, followed by the skipper name. *Chatham* Frank, *Dixie* Don, *Chanty* Ken. I hate that everyone calls Dad *Squiddly* George. But it's bad luck to change the name of a boat, so he must have expected it when he bought the *Squid*. It's also bad luck to have bananas on board, whistle in the wheelhouse, and leave town on a Friday, but we've done all those things at some point. If he did change the name, he says it would be the F/V *Alyce* and then he'd be *Alyce* George, and that's not much better.

I listen to Dad and *Sunshine* Sam speak their strange boat language.

"Oh yeah . . ." Long pause. Interminably long pause. "Yep, Marty over at the Cape." Long, long pause. "Twenty-two pounder . . ."

"Huh . . ." Long pause.

"'S that when he gaffed his own leg?"

It's like speaking in code.

"You going to dance for me?" Uncle Gorky hands me a mug of tea.

I shrug, sliding into boat-speak as easy as pulling on my rain gear. Dad is unrolling charts and plotting our course, a bit more focused than usual, as if it's the first time we've ever left the harbor. I know he heard Uncle Gorky's question, but you'd never know it by looking at him.

I watch his calloused finger move along the nautical chart. He's trying to decide which direction to go—the best place to anchor that's protected in case the weather kicks up, but still close to the fishing grounds. We are running now, a day early, so we can get the gear in the water right when the season opens. Every minute spent getting to the fishing grounds is money lost. Dad likes to have the hooks in the water right at midnight on July first, opening day.

The chart he's reading is creased from wear and there is Scotch tape holding it in spots that tore over time. Some of the bays on the chart are covered in coffee stains, or crusted with dried salt from my father's wet gloves, the paper crinkled where it was gripped too tight during a storm. I notice a dried spot of blood marking Murder Cove, a safe, secluded bay with a horrible name. That purplish spot bruising the chart could be fish blood, or blood from a hand that got stuck with a hook, or just blood from a bloody nose. The older the charts get, the more history they contain.

The names of the bays tell their own stories, and some

have given me nightmares over the years—just knowing we were anchored in places called Murder Cove or Deadman's Reach, or even running against fifty-knot winds through a strait ominously named Peril. Whoever decided on these names was trying to tell us something. I prefer the hand-written notes beside other bays and landmarks inked in Uncle Gorky's familiar scrawl: "good anchorage," or "caught 10 halibut on a hand line," or "Dungeness crab—*lots!*"

It's considered really bad manners to snoop and read other mariner's charts. It's the closest thing to a journal for men who trust no one but the sea. If you happen to climb aboard another boat and their chart is lying out on the table, you better not get caught looking directly at it. Men have been thrown overboard just for glancing.

Dad unrolls another chart and spreads it out, tracing the route we'll take today. Scribbled in the margin of a passage along a narrow stretch, my mother's tight, bossy handwriting jumps out at me: "Right on red returning." It's the most basic nautical rule of them all.

I point to it and nudge Dad's shoulder.

He tugs at his whiskers, which is what he always does any time the subject of my mother comes up, or worse, if he has to talk to her himself. Once he came back from the pay phone at the top of the dock with whole sections of his mustache pulled out.

Luckily, Uncle Gorky jumps in when he sees that gesture: Dad ripping his hair out.

"Uh, someone almost hit a rock there. Thought the marker

was in the wrong place." A smile lurks at the corner of his mouth. He tries to hide it, lifting his mug and slurping tea louder than necessary.

Oh, Mom, I think. *You documented your most serious fishing blunder on the chart?* She might as well have written it on her tombstone.

We're slowly crawling out of town at just a little over four knots. Through the window I can see the other boat harbor, and just beyond it the ferry terminal on the starboard side as we pass.

Once we're past the harbor bathroom, I let out the air I've been holding, aware that Uncle Gorky is watching me, smiling. It's a game a bunch of us fishing kids made up a long time ago, the equivalent of holding your breath and making a wish while driving over a bridge. I don't really know why, but the rumor is that the bathroom is haunted. My parents said that was ridiculous and refused to even hear about it.

"And even if it was, how is holding your breath going to help?" Mom had asked, and Dad agreed. (Oddly, it was one of the few things they absolutely agreed on, and they got equally annoyed when I talked about it.)

I figure it's no different from all the other superstitions fishermen live by. I mean, seriously, if bananas are dangerous on a boat, can't a bathroom be haunted?

* * *

The M/V *Matanuska* is tied up at the ferry terminal, but I can see them loading cars onto her as we go by. She'll probably pass us since the most the *Squid* can do is eight knots, and a huge ferry goes way faster than that. It'll rock us around in its wake, so Dad is busy putting dishes in the drawers and cleaning off the table. I glance up at the dried oatmeal that's still on the ceiling from another trip when things went flying in the wake of a ferry, combined with some nasty weather. If Mom were still on the boat, she'd probably go apeshit because nobody's bothered to clean it up, but I think Dad and Uncle Gorky use it as a reminder to put things away. Or maybe she's right and they're just lazy.

I can feel my frustration about not being able to dance start to slip away, even though part of me wants to hold on to it—to roll it around like a hard little stone in my pocket, mine and mine alone.

Even if I do wish I could dance, it smells so much better in this part of Alaska, thanks to the minty Tongass rain forest with its huge cedars and hemlocks and all its lush greenery. Up north the skinny black spruce trees look like they're constantly trying to fill their lungs, their roots suffocating underground in permafrost. Same state, two climates, each as different as my parents; and like my parents, there's a part of me in both.

"Dad, I'm going up on the flying bridge." I grab my life jacket on the way out. I want to practice that last combination we learned just before I left so I don't forget it.

On the flying bridge the smells are even stronger, trying to draw me out of myself. Salt and mint and fish and wind, mingled with diesel. My arms and legs relax, as if they are made of moss. I used to pretend my parents found me in the rain forest, a magical creature born of spongy muskeg and old man's beard. It seems almost possible now as I spin around a couple times, trying to get my sea legs, feeling the rhythm of the boat making its own dance.

And there she is, the *Pelican,* my inflatable blue raft that has been my best friend on this boat every summer of my life. She knows me better than anyone, and when I climb inside her my whole body relaxes and I can hear her whisper how happy she is that I am back. I drift slowly off to sleep.

A while later I wake up groggy and not sure where I am, feeling the *Squid* pounding beneath the wake of another boat. The *Matanuska* ferry is passing us, and nearby is a pod of orcas, closer than I've ever seen them get to a boat that large. And then I see something else that shouldn't be there. Even if I yelled, no one would hear me. It isn't until it's too late that my voice finally finds its way out of my throat, but by then I can't tell whether it's me or the orcas that are screaming.

CHAPTER FOUR

Chasing Orcas

HANK

If I didn't believe that people we love are still taking care of us after they die, I wouldn't be sitting here now, hugging my knees, surrounded by baggage, trying not to wiggle or sneeze. Fourteen-year-old Jack is asleep with his head lying against a canvas army bag with a Seattle address—looking for all the world like he sleeps every day of his life in a baggage cart bound for the lower forty-eight. My other brother, Sam, is sixteen, just a year younger than me; but he's a dreamy, innocent sixteen, so naive it scares me sometimes. He's not as relaxed as Jack at the moment, maybe because his long legs barely fit in the cart and he's pulled them up to his chin. Also because he's not so sure stowing away on the ferry was a very good idea.

But we're doing it anyway, stowing away on the M/V *Matanuska*. And before you start wondering if my elevator doesn't go all the way to the top floor, I should say right now that between me and Jack and Sam, I'm not only the oldest, I'm also the most levelheaded.

"Will we still be able to go out on deck and look for orcas?" Sam asked, as if he needed a better excuse than just getting away from my mother's awful boyfriend, Nathan Hodges.

I don't want to talk bad about my mom. I mean, I think she waited around for a while, hoping maybe Dad wasn't really dead, but she gave up a lot sooner than me and definitely sooner than Sam.

At some point I noticed Mom started looking tired all the time, and I realized she'd been sneaking out every night, hooking up with someone. In hindsight, the sneaking out was a lot better than bringing the guy home. I couldn't believe it the first time I saw him. Nathan Hodges was short and squat, with stubby legs and Neanderthal arms, and fat sausage fingers. He gripped his beer can so tight, one hand could cover all but the last *r* in *Budweiser*. So, looks aren't everything, but instead of words he grunted out commands that Mom jumped up to follow, and then he slapped her on the ass as she walked by. And it didn't help that Nathan Hodges had some kind of grudge against Jack, which Mom seemed powerless to do anything about. How does someone go from being a decent mother and having a husband who treats her like a queen to bringing home the first mangy stray dog she finds on the street?

"You're too young, Hank," she said to me, the one time I asked her what the hell she was doing. "You wait until your whole world falls out from under you."

"My world *is* falling out from under me," I said.

"Your dad was a great guy, but he was never home. You boys have him on a pedestal because that's what kids do around here. They all have these romantic notions of the mysterious dad out fishing, while the women stay home and do all the work. It's easy to make a martyr out of the guy who goes and gets himself killed. I'm just another fishing widow, left with a bunch of mouths to feed."

She was looking deep into her cup of Hills Bros. coffee. As if that cup of coffee was the only thing in the world that understood her now. At that moment, I kind of hated her for being the one who lived. I'm ashamed to admit it, but there you go.

"At least I got a guy who comes home every night," she said, like she was a deflated balloon that had been flying around the room with a slow leak and was relieved to just finally land.

"Right," I said, "because that seems to be working out real well for all of us."

I pretty much avoided her after that, which wasn't as hard as you might think. It hurt to hear her say my dad wasn't what I'd thought he'd been. It nagged at me for days, like a splinter under the skin. So it was no surprise when I ended up in the garage going through my dad's old boxes, trying to get a better picture of the man I couldn't stop missing.

The boxes smelled like my dad's aftershave, Old Spice. I thought maybe a bottle of it had gotten shoved in somewhere, underneath his old news clippings or the fishing magazines with huge glossy covers of rugged, bearded men holding up halibut as big as them. Dad was a news junkie and he saved everything. But no aftershave bottle.

There was stuff about the territorial governor and the statehood commission. I forgot that when we were born Alaska was still a territory. There was the headline from 1959—"We're In"—and I could almost hear my dad's voice saying sadly, "That's sure going to change things."

I wished I could ask him what he'd meant and if it was different now. But everything really was different now. I couldn't blame statehood, but if there was a way, I'd consider it.

Jack had come in just then and said, "What's that smell?"

"It's Old Spice," I said. Jack had been too young to remember what our father smelled like.

"It's creepy," Jack said. "Feels like someone's in here."

"Stop it, Jack."

My brother has this really weird streak—like a sixth sense. Sometimes Sam and I will joke about it, but I didn't find it funny just then with my dad's stuff all around us and his very distinct smell lingering like a ghost. Jack raised an eyebrow at me and shrugged.

He knows more than any fourteen-year-old kid should know about people. It has the unfortunate effect of making me want to leap up and protect him all the time, because I don't think the world knows what to do with people like Jack.

"I've been reading through the newspaper and cutting out stories," he said. "You know, the way Dad used to."

Jack picks up on things easily. He knew that Sam and I missed this seemingly insignificant detail about our dad— the way he saved news clippings—and so he'd try to do something about it. "Look at this," he said, showing me an article he'd clipped out. It was already two months old.

> *May 5, 1970, Fairbanks: The tripod on the Nenana River fell at exactly 10:37 a.m. yesterday to mark the end of the 1970 Nenana Ice Classic and signal the beginning of spring. Five lucky winners will split the $10,000 pot. One of the five is a sixteen-year-old native girl, who has asked not to be identified. She is the youngest winner yet for the Ice Classic tournament, which was started as a betting pool in 1906 as a way for miners to entertain themselves in anticipation of the spring breakup.*

"She's going to get two thousand dollars, that girl is," Jack said. "That's a hell of a lot of money."

Jack isn't a jealous person, but he was obviously jealous about this.

"Jack?" I said. "What would you do with all that money?"

"I'd leave," he said, without even thinking about it. "I'd take that money and I'd get on a ferry and I'd leave."

Right about then the window blew open, banging against

the garage wall and making us both jump. A cold wind started blowing all the old newspapers and receipts around the garage. It sounded like the flapping of a hundred invisible wings whipping up the last bits of my dad, trying to resurrect him. When the dust settled, all I could smell was that Old Spice aftershave, and right then I knew I had to listen to Jack.

"Let's go," I said to him. "Let's get Sam and let's go."

"We won't have to stay hidden the whole time, if that's what you're asking," I told Sam in answer to his question about looking for whales. "But I think it's rare to see orcas."

Sam remembered every single fishing story Dad ever told us. I could hear my mother's voice in my head—*you boys think those fishing stories are so mysterious and romantic, always keeping him up on a pedestal*—but I pushed it away and thought about what Dad told us instead, about the time he was longlining for black cod. The baited lines sit on the bottom of the ocean for a few hours, then get pulled up by hydraulics, hopefully loaded with fish. By the time they were pulling in the gear, orcas had totally surrounded the boat.

"Gorgeous animals," Dad said. "So quick, so powerful. They can pull bait right off the gear. The only thing left on the hook after we pulled in the line was a pair of black cod lips."

Sam hung on to the stories like the lips had hung on to the hook, and he could recite every single one, even though it's been years since Dad disappeared.

Sam was the poet, the one who would keep Dad alive regardless of the facts. Those facts included his entire boat being swallowed in a tsunami. The one that hit right after the Good Friday earthquake had rocked the rest of the state— houses broke in half and slid into the bay in Anchorage; broken roads twisted all the way from Valdez to Turnagain Arm. But hundreds of miles away from the epicenter, it was the ocean that wreaked havoc, swallowing a whole fleet of boats, including our father's.

I had begged him to take me on that particular trip to Massacre Bay. I was eleven. It was his favorite place to fish because the mountains jutted straight out of the ocean. "It feels like they're hugging your boat and keeping you safe while you pull in the fish," he'd said. I could not imagine a place called Massacre Bay feeling safe and secure like a hug. And I was right about that, wasn't I?

I've never been able to shake that feeling of Dad's hand on top of my head, ruffling my hair while he said, "You stay home and be the man of the house for me this one time. There will be other trips."

I didn't realize that being the man of the house was going to get so goddamn tiring.

Hiding in the baggage cart is getting tiring as well, but since we didn't win a pot of money like that girl in Fairbanks, it was the only way I could think of to sneak aboard. Thank God people have so much baggage when they leave Alaska.

Just in this cart alone there are duffel bags, suitcases, boxes of frozen salmon, padded gun cases—and us. I move a box covered in duct tape closer to my left foot, trying to hide my legs. The shutters on the cart open and a wave of yellow sunlight bounces off my shoelaces. I hold my breath as someone pushes a cage in nearly on top of my foot. Inside it four mustard-brown hens squawk loudly. *You have got to be kidding me.*

"They'll be so lonely. Are you sure I can't take them above deck with me?" a woman's voice says.

Sam's mouth crinkles around the edges and I'm afraid he's going to laugh. Jack stretches and yawns loudly, but the chickens are squawking so much, nobody is going to hear anything over that racket. I relax a little as the ferryman leads the woman away. We can still hear her high, protesting voice, and apparently so can her chickens, which call out to her in a chorus of mad clucks that luckily drown out Sam's laughter.

"Hush, Sam—" The cart is starting to move down the ramp.

The car deck is a sensory overload of diesel, mold, and exhaust from all the vehicles. Jack wakes and tries to stretch, then looks around, disoriented. I press a finger to my lips and he stops moving. Jack nods and stays quiet. He is so easy. Unlike Sam, who is already giving me a can-we-please-get-off-this-thing-now kind of look. I'd really like to get as far away from town as possible before we show ourselves to the general public. That way there will be less of a chance of getting sent back if we get caught. If we could at least make it to Ketchikan or Prince Rupert, in Canada, that would be okay. All I found in my mom's peanut butter jar was sixteen dollars, and I'm no idiot. That's almost like having no money at all. I just want to be somewhere else before I worry about every single detail. We got this far, didn't we?

A million tiny needles dance under my skin all the way down to my toes, and I realize Sam is shaking my leg, which is fast asleep.

"I'm getting a headache from this diesel smell," he whispers. "And there's going to be a car deck call soon. People are going to come get their bags. We have to get out of here anyway."

He's right. We've done this trip enough to know the basics, even if it was a long time ago. Our parents brought tents and we camped up on the solarium. Jack was probably two or three; I doubt he remembers. It's weird to think about how much stuff we brought along back then. Dad had to go back and forth to the car to get the cooler, the sleeping bags, the tent, and shopping bags full of food. This time all we've got is the sixteen dollars and two coats apiece, which we're wearing in layers on our backs. At least it's summer, but we can probably sleep inside in the forward lounge anyway, where it's warmer.

Sam squeezes my arm and I nod in agreement. Time to make a move.

We slip out the back of the cart and slink behind the parked cars with blocks shoved under their front wheels to keep them from moving. We lurch from side to side, trying to find some kind of rhythm with the sway of the boat. Sea legs take a while, and ours are still asleep.

The chicken lady sits hunched in the stairwell, her head in her hands. She's waiting for the announcement saying it's okay to go below deck. The way her frizzy gray hair hangs over her face makes her look like a mossy spruce tree, bent with age.

"Your chickens are fine," Jack says without thinking. She looks straight through him like he's not even there.

We go up to the bow and sit facing the wind, gladly trading diesel fumes for salt air, even if it does take our breath away. Sam scans the horizon for whales.

"I'm hungry," says Jack.

"I know." I've been dreading this moment.

"Let's wait a little longer. We can get some leftovers once people leave their trays."

Jack wrinkles his nose.

"We have to save our money," I tell him. "You'll see. People just leave perfectly good things. Sometimes they don't even touch it if they're seasick or whatever. It'll be fine."

"I want to stay and look for whales. You guys go ahead," says Sam, staring out at the ocean.

"We have to always stick together, Sam," I say. "And if possible, we need to look like we're with parents. Just sit close to people so it doesn't look like we're all alone."

"I can't miss the whales," he says. God, is he going to be this frustrating the whole time?

But his voice tugs at something inside of me, that long-abandoned belief that my father might really come back. For Sam, Dad and the whales are one and the same. I'm a tiny bit envious that he still gets to have that. "All right, we'll bring you some food. Stay right here, Sam. I mean it."

So Jack and I steer ourselves past the purser's station, looking for all the world like any other normal, paying passengers. Except maybe puffier, because of our extra coats. I hear a *twang, twang, twang* behind me and turn to see Jack playing with something in his hand. "What is that?"

He holds a skanky red rubber band in my face. It smells like shit.

"Where did you get that?" I cover my nose.

"One of those hens was pecking at it inside the cage. I was able to grab it through the wires."

"You'll get a disease from that thing," I say.

"I think it's a good-luck charm." His face is all lit up with possibility. Remember when I said I was the most level-headed one in my family? If we survive this journey, it will be nothing short of a miracle, thanks to my brothers, who are starting to make me very nervous.

"I'll go give it to Sam," Jack says. "It might help bring in the whales."

In spite of myself, I smile watching Jack run back to where Sam is still rooted to the deck. There's Sam, still hoping Dad will come back, and Jack, trying to help find ways to make it so. What I feel is a mix of crazy love and jealousy—for both of them. And even after everything Jack's been through, he still believes in good-luck charms. Did I stop believing in everything all at once, or was it so gradual I just didn't notice?

"You are absolutely washing those hands before we get food, even leftover food," I tell him when he gets back. He smiles one of those break-your-heart-every-day kind of smiles, like he feels sorry for me because I have no imagination, but heads into the men's room.

The dining hall looks just like it did when we were here before. The long line at the buffet counter, the man flipping burgers at the grill in the little blue boater hat, and the sound of popping grease in the fryer. The smell is enough to make me waste money on our very first day. I realize we haven't eaten in almost twenty-four hours, since we sneaked out around midnight and dinner was our last meal. Dinner, as in bowls of cereal before going to bed fully dressed. Mom and Nathan came home from the bar and I thought they'd never stop fighting. I could see the whites of Jack's eyes staring up at the ceiling. I realized then that Jack rarely slept at night. It's why I used to find him curled up in the oddest places in the middle of the day, sound asleep. We should have left a long time ago.

I can tell Jack doesn't like my plan. He's staring at the plates left on the tables, a disgusted look on his face. This is the same kid who just ten minutes ago was holding a rubber band covered in chicken shit and telling me it was lucky.

"I have money, Hank, I'll buy us food," he says as I inspect a whole banana, more brown than yellow but still in its peel.

I put it in the plastic bag I brought along just for this reason. My planning skills are minimal, but I did think of a few things. I toss in half a bag of chips and a chicken leg that looks totally untouched. I leave the gross, soggy hamburger drowning in ketchup.

"You don't have money, Jack. Where would you have gotten money?"

Just then the cashier eyes us suspiciously and I pull Jack along by his coat toward the other end of the cafeteria. If we just keep our heads down, hopefully it'll take a while before we stand out, maybe forever—we look almost normal compared to some of the rough-looking passengers. We steer clear of a guy with a skullcap dressed all in black leather. The girl he's with has a raven tattooed on her cheek, and she appears to be wearing a sleeping bag. Her bare feet are sticking out of the side zipper, making her look like a puffy mermaid.

Jack grabs a Parmesan cheese container from the condiment rack and tips it back into his mouth like a drunken sailor. *Good Lord, Jack, really?*

Back on deck, Sam is nowhere to be found. Have we been gone that long? Jack seems unconcerned as he munches on the chicken leg. He seems to have gotten over his phobia about the meal plan. We circle the boat, stem to stern, my adrenaline picking up with every passing minute. Why did I leave him out here alone? I notice the chicken lady standing almost exactly where we last saw Sam. She's clutching the railing and the wind is whipping her hair into a cylinder shape on top of her head, like it's being sucked up by a vacuum.

"My brother," I say to her, "he was standing right here, looking for whales. Did you see him?"

She sniffs the air. As she turns, her hair rockets skyward and the wind grabs it and whips it in the opposite direction as if an invisible puppeteer is operating from above. It would be comical if I weren't so worried about Sam.

"Did you see my brother?" I am inches from her face. She says nothing and I grab her by the shoulders, gently shaking her into focus. It's like holding on to a cobweb. At first I think she's going to disintegrate right in my hands, but then she grabs my cheeks and pulls me right up to her face. Her breath is old and dusty. "Nobody knows what it's like to be you. Nobody! Do you hear me?"

I close my eyes. I can feel Jack without even seeing him. He has thrown his arms around the woman's waist and he's hugging her so tight, it slowly makes her loosen her grip and drop her fingers from my burning cheeks. I hear Jack's voice shushing her. "It's all right. It's all right. It's all right."

If this is the only person who saw what happened to Sam, we are in trouble. I doubt she will ever be able to tell us anything. Suddenly I am the one made of thin, wispy cobwebs, in danger of blowing away bit by bit.

CHAPTER FIVE

Shoot for the Stars

RUTH

After Dora won the Ice Classic, a lot of kids in Birch Park started getting ideas. If she could win, then maybe it was possible that other kids from our neighborhood could get a lucky break, too. Everybody wanted to grab on tight and hitch a ride on the skirts of Dora's success. But I wasn't fooled.

I had been right about holding my breath and not believing when something is too good to be true. Gran found Ray's white T-shirt and threw it in the wash, not knowing at all whose it was or what it meant. The smell of cedar was completely washed out of it by the time I heard that he was dating Della May, one of the new girls who had moved up from Outside. I had been too embarrassed to face Mrs. Stevens again, and Ray let me know pretty quickly that he wanted a girlfriend who would sleep over, not one who just talked on the telephone late at night.

At first I told Gran that I probably had the flu, which I hoped was true. After a while I knew it couldn't be that—I'm pretty sure she did, too, but she said nothing—not even when I stole a whole box of saltines and took them to school to keep in my locker.

Ray would walk by sometimes and act like we'd never even met. He and Della May sounded like a bad country western song, and she always walked with her arm linked through his, as if she might suddenly end up back in Texas if she wasn't tethered to him every second. *There are worse things that could happen to you,* I thought, but who was I to warn her?

She had a funny accent, and when she said his name she'd drag the *A* out so long, I could hear it even after they'd turned the corner by the broken water fountain.

Then I'd stare at the water fountain, wishing it had magical powers and would bubble up a secret potion that I could drink and my life could go back in time. I'd even settle for just as far back as that swim meet—when he flicked me on the butt with a towel and asked me to come to a party—so I could say no. But this broken fountain hadn't even bubbled up water the entire time I'd been at this school, so obviously anything more would be asking a lot.

Even now I had no plan for the future, except that I knew I was never going to tell Ray what was happening. I had to do this all on my own—somehow—because I wasn't going to trust anyone else ever, ever again.

Luckily the school year ended and my secret was still small enough that I'd managed to hide it from everyone, even Selma. I spent the first part of summer break sleeping. I could almost convince myself that I was Sleeping Beauty, and if I just managed to stay unconscious for the next few months maybe I'd wake up and be a whole new person. I didn't know it then, but in a way, that's what was going to happen; I just didn't realize how far from a fairy tale it was going to be.

"Are you sure you should eat all that Spam *and* a bowl of Cap'n Crunch *and* three pieces of peanut butter toast?" Lily asks one morning. "You're getting kind of fat, Ruth."

"Well, that's a nice thing to say," I answer, shoving the whole slab of disgusting pink fake meat into my mouth and glaring at her.

"Suit yourself. But Bunny said something about it the other day," she goes on. "She said even Dora has noticed."

Well, isn't that great? Dora, whose entire life was on display, nightgown and all, has decided it's okay to talk about my weight? Maybe she thinks we've all forgotten that scene between her and her dad, now that she's won the Ice Classic?

I feel myself start to shake. Lately I can get worked up

about nothing. But this isn't nothing. Of all people, Dora Peters is talking about me? So, now that she has money and a nice cozy home, I suppose I'm fair game, am I? I can just picture her over at Dumpling and Bunny's, all of them sitting around the table and Dumpling's mother making sourdough pancakes and venison sausage; I can smell the food they eat from the merry-go-round. Actually, I can smell food from almost anywhere these days. I have never been jealous of those girls before, but I can feel it rearing its ugly green head. I wish I could be *anyone* but me—even Dora—which means I've really hit rock bottom.

I want to jump up and yell, "Lily, you dumb shit, I'm pregnant!"

Why not? Gran is at the sink, pretending that her ears have fallen off and she's blind as a bat. Suddenly she can't see anything that's happening to me, when she used to watch me like a hawk. How ironic that the bigger I get, the more invisible I become.

Except that I overheard her on the telephone, making a reservation for a bus ride to Canada under my name.

I could see how Lily might be absolutely clueless, considering she doesn't even understand the difference between her and Bunny, but Gran? I had no idea that the silent treatment could be so much worse than public humiliation. Gran has more than one trick up her sleeve.

When I get up and head out the door, I pause, wondering if she'll ask me where I'm going or when I'm coming back. The only sound in the room is Gran's yellow dish gloves squeaking as she rubs the soapy sponge across a plate. She says nothing. When I leave I make sure to slam the screen door extra hard, and still she doesn't come out. I am officially not even worth reprimanding.

I walk all the way to the Salvation Army without looking up, not at the river or the little white church where my parents got married, and not at Crazy Dancing Guy who is strangely silent when I pass. It's one of those hot summer days that smells smoky from distant wildfires, and I am sticky with sweat by the time I push through the Salvation Army's jingly door.

I need to buy some bigger clothes. Dora's mother is there with some of her friends, and when I pass them in the aisle, well, let's just say they did not go to the Gran school of feigned obliviousness.

"Someone's got a bun in the oven," one of them chortles.

I don't look up; I just push my cart slowly between them. I stop and pretend to admire a rack of long woolen underwear. A person can never have enough long underwear.

"Remember those days, Paula?" The woman talks loudly, as if Paula is a hundred miles away instead of right next to her, holding a fuzzy toilet-seat cover that looks like it was made out of a poodle.

"You was jealous then, girl, don't try to lie. Alvin got his daddy's nice station wagon for the weekend and he put that mattress back in there."

They are laughing so hard, I inch slowly away, trying not to get caught in between the memory of someone named Alvin and his daddy's car.

"I was not jealous. You coulda got frostbit back there 'cause the heater broke. You forget that?"

"Remember you was gonna name the baby Frosty the Snowman?" Dora's mom chimes in, and they all explode in a fit of giggles.

I cannot imagine talking so freely about what I did with Ray. And it wasn't in the back of some car on a freezing cold night. It had meant something.

Right up until it didn't. For him. I hate the feeling that this is exactly what you hear about. How nothing changes for the guy. I am a cliché and a statistic all in one. And nothing says that louder than this moment, standing in the Salvation Army completely alone, looking for clothes that six of my closest friends probably could have all fit into at once. Except I don't have six close friends. I'm getting close to having no friends at all.

Is Ray letting Della May sneak into his room, I wonder? Does she look out at the lake and then go home with the smell of cedar in her hair?

I put my face into a gray hoodie with an orange basketball etched on the front and breathe in the smell of someone else. Someone named Lucy, according to the name embroidered on the front of it. Over the top of the basketball it says SHOOT FOR THE STARS, and it smells like sweat and mildew. But that's better than cedar. If I ever smell cedar again, I will probably throw up.

"Are you okay, young lady?"

I look up into the face of the oldest man I've ever seen. And for the first time since Ray's mom looked at me with her sad blue eyes, I feel like someone is actually seeing me—not my face or my widening belly, but the me that I've become since my parents left, since Gran cut off my hair, and since I realized that my life was never going to be the same again.

An hour later, I'm still sitting in the back room at the Salvation Army, my face puffy from crying, and George, the crinkly-faced manager, has given me a doughnut and some Swiss Miss cocoa. In between customers, he keeps coming back to check on me. He doesn't say anything, just pats me on the shoulder or hands me a tissue, then goes back out to ring up sales.

"Want me to call someone?" he finally says after checking on me four or five times. His voice wraps around me like a warm bath and I'm afraid I'll start crying all over again, just when I've finally managed to pull myself together. "How about your friend with those big brown eyes?"

"You remember us?" Selma and I shop here sometimes after school, but we had never really paid attention to George before. It seems rude now, after how nice he's been to me.

"I ain't seen eyes like that since my seal-hunting days," he says. His own eyes are the size of two tiny black apple seeds, and yet they look right through me.

I just nod at him, but I do not want to call Selma. Who, by the way, would be thrilled to know George thinks she has eyes like a seal. Ironically, that's what we were fighting about, on the surface anyway. Selma was going on and on about how her real mother was probably a selkie, one of those half-human, half-seal creatures that can take off their skin and walk out of the ocean during the full moon. This can't possibly be true, but Selma loves to fantasize about anything that might give her story an air of mystery. The reality is that she never met her parents, and Abigail, her mom, doesn't like to talk about it. Maybe she doesn't know who Selma's parents are, but she's not really forthcoming with the details.

It's one of the things Selma and I have in common: not knowing what happened to our mothers. But I'm fed up with Selma's ridiculous make-believe stories. It was fine when she was ten, but now it's just childish.

Mostly, my emotions are kind of all over the place these days. So it's better if I just shut everyone out.

"No thanks," I tell George, "I don't really want to call anyone."

I also cannot imagine walking out of this office. I want to stay here for a hundred years, or until I eat so many doughnuts I no longer fit through the door.

But of course, I do walk out into the dusty June day about an hour later with a bag full of free clothes, because George refused to let me pay. I'm wearing the basketball hoodie and hoping maybe I can somehow evolve into this "Lucy" person and leave Ruth behind. Whoever she was, she wasn't tiny, and we've at least got that in common.

At the little white church, I stop and sit down on the steps to watch the river meander by. It's still pretty high after the spring melt. A statue of the Virgin Mary is off to my left, her hands folded over her blue gown. "How did you get them all to believe it was a virgin birth?" I ask her, but of course she doesn't answer. I notice that her eyes are cast off to the side, as if to deflect questions like this from girls like me.

My parents were married in this church, but we never went to Mass until we moved in with Gran. My parents called themselves "lapsed Catholics," and when I was younger I thought it meant they ran laps around Catholics.

That doesn't even make any sense.

I have an early memory of my mother and father whispering together when they thought I was asleep. Our house was so tiny I slept on their floor, in a makeshift bed my father built out of camping pads and thick woolen blankets. I liked to hear them talking in their secret adult language, which lulled me to sleep every night. But as I get older, the words that seemed random and foreign then have grown more recognizable. I can now string them together like a family heirloom that hangs around my neck, almost strangling me. Words like *rules, suffocating, serious, guilt,* and *sin.*

"Thank you for saving me from that," Mama whispered, and I realize now she meant Gran. My father saved her, but there's nobody left to save me and Lily. I think about the baby growing inside me. If I can't save myself, how can I ever save someone else?

I know Gran has probably already made all the arrangements for this baby to be adopted. Will it hate me?

I'm so lost in my own thoughts that I hardly notice Dumpling, who has come up and is now sitting on the steps next to me. I like Dumpling, but we don't hang out or walk together or sit on the merry-go-round at Birch Park, like she and Dora do. We usually don't sit on the steps of churches together, either. I glance over at her, because I'm sure she knows this, too, but she just shrugs and looks out at the river.

It's surprisingly nice. I can feel myself relaxing and soon I'm not just stealing glances at her, but really looking. She has a long black braid tied at the bottom with a red ribbon. I'm surprised at how familiar that ribbon is to me. I guess when you walk behind someone for as many years as I have, there are things you don't even realize you're noticing.

I'm also struck by the way Dumpling doesn't resemble her name at all. Maybe I'd never really looked at her properly. She is slim and beautiful, with the most amazing olive skin and almond-shaped eyes. Her black hair shines like oil in the late afternoon sun.

Suddenly I want to tell her everything. But all I manage to say is "I'll be getting sent away soon."

"Really? Why?"

"Isn't it obvious?" I say. "I'm a disgrace to my family."

"I wouldn't say that at all," she says. "Isn't there an auntie or someone who would want to raise your baby?"

She says "your baby" as if it's not a horrible ugly secret but just a fact. Maybe even something sweet.

"Do people do that?"

"Where we come from, babies are a gift to the whole village. Everyone loves them."

"I can see why Lily is dying to be Athabascan," I say.

Dumpling just laughs. "It would be easier for Lily if she was, I guess."

"Really? Even though people talk about you?"

But maybe Dumpling doesn't know this. I look away, embarrassed at saying too much.

"Does all this talk come from the same people who would send you away for something as silly as this?" she asks, pointing to my belly.

She has a good point, so I shut up. For a few minutes it feels like we are standing on opposite banks of the same river.

After a while, almost as if she is reading my mind, Dumpling asks in a quiet whisper, "Remember the flood?"

The flood, I think, and of course I remember it. It was years ago, but I can still hear the sound of the river—too close, too fast. The skiff picking us up on the doorstep of Gran's house, the sound of the outboard. The smell of fuel. I remember seeing a dead baby moose float past. You can't unsee something like that once you've seen it, no matter how hard you try. It had deep brown eyes and huge paintbrush lashes, just like Selma's.

Less than an hour ago, George said Selma's eyes reminded him of a seal, and now I'm comparing them to a moose. I would laugh if it didn't make me suddenly miss her.

Selma, who had been so stoic about getting shots with a humongous needle during the flood. It had impressed me. I wanted her as a friend because she was unlike anyone I'd ever met. But I don't say any of this to Dumpling when she asks if I remember the flood. I just say, "Sort of."

Dumpling smiles. But she's already back there, I can tell. And when she speaks again I can hear the sound of the river in her voice.

It's not civilized for a river to jump its banks. It's like having a friend turn on you, and I see Ray's face as I think this. I rub my belly and think about how clueless I've been about things like babies and floods, and all the other ways the world might turn uncivilized when you least expect it.

"My dad put us all in the skiff," Dumpling is saying. "We were headed to the high school like everyone else, but there wasn't room for all of us in one boat. So my mom stayed behind. I waved to her as we pulled out and watched her get smaller and smaller, like a tiny planet that was suddenly a million miles away."

This is the most I've ever heard Dumpling say at one time.

"All kinds of things floated past us: gas jugs, rubber boots, old tires. There was an entire refrigerator with its door swung open, spilling out ketchup and mustard and jars of pickles right next to the library, when it was in that old cabin on First Avenue. Do you remember that?"

I do, but I'm thinking about the refrigerator with all of its secrets spilled out for the world to see, like the hookers who used to flash little bits of themselves just one block away. We used to go to the log cabin library on First Avenue, and like the flood, sometimes the hookers jumped their banks and strolled too far south, and we would catch a glimpse of a fishnet stocking, or the flash of a feather boa peeking out from under a parka.

"Then we passed a red silk slip, stuck in a fence."

Wait. I remember this, too. "We laughed at that," I tell her. "All of us. Gran got so mad, I thought she was going to smack us."

"Really?" Dumpling says. "You remember it?"

I nod, wondering who it might have belonged to and what had happened to her. Was it one of the Second Avenue hookers? They had never seemed like real people when we were kids, just part of the scenery. Little girls stayed on First Avenue at the library, with our picture books and quiet voices, and the hookers and drunks stayed on Second, like a movie that stayed on a screen; everyone in their places.

I can see this clearly now, from where we sit on the steps of the little white church. If you don't follow the rules—even one single time—there might be floods and earthquakes, or worse.

"I thought it was so fancy," Dumpling is saying, "I pointed it out to my dad and he got this huge grin. 'Your mother would look like a beautiful salmon in that,' he said. My dad loves salmon." She smiles as if the memory is a peppermint stick and she's licking it, slowly savoring every bit.

"He dropped us at the high school and then went back to get my mom. The National Guard told him it was too dangerous—not to go back because the current had picked up. He wouldn't listen."

"But your mom was safe. She'd already been rescued, right?" I know she's fine because she's here, and yet I can feel my heart racing along with Dumpling's story.

She shakes her head. Her pupils have turned from brown to black pools of muddy water that look like they're watching her mother drown over and over again. "She was trapped in the basement and he had to swim to her and then pull her out. She was unconscious and he just kept pressing on her chest and blowing air into her nose. He said she finally spouted water out of her mouth and he was so happy, he wanted to drown her again in kisses."

"He really loves her that much?" I ask, before I can stop myself.

"Yeah" is all Dumpling says. Then, "He grabbed the red silk slip out of the fence on his way back to the high school, but my mother was horrified by it."

I look closer at the red ribbon in her hair. I honestly cannot imagine Dumpling's mother—who is round and plump like a loaf of bread—wearing anything like that slip. But I don't say this.

"I held on to it. Because of the way he said she'd look in it, like a beautiful salmon. I've never told anyone before," she says.

"Did you cut it up?" I ask, resisting the urge to reach out and touch her ribbon.

"A bunch of little strips," she says. "I have a whole cigar box full of them. I figure it's good luck. You know, a reminder of what love can do."

"And if he had died?" I ask. "Or she had died?"

"I'd still have saved it," she says. "Because sometimes you just have to hold on to whatever you can."

Dumpling takes the ribbon out of her hair and hands it to me. "For you, *Lucy*," she says, smiling and pointing to the name on my sweatshirt. "This one's extra-long so you can cut it and give half to your baby."

I'm holding the scraggly ribbon in my hand and I'm so afraid I'll start crying, I say nothing.

"It works," she says, "I promise."

And then she gets up and walks away with a slight wave of her hand.

How does it work? I wonder. But the next time I look up she is already just a tiny speck in the distance, like a planet that is a million miles away.

CHAPTER SIX

Fish Camp

DORA

Winning the Ice Classic was both the best and worst thing that could happen to a girl like me. In between dreaming about all the things I could buy with that money—like new boots, thick woolen socks, and cherry-dipped cones whenever I wanted—there was the huge overriding fear that this would make my parents and their friends very interested in me.

It reminded me of a poem we read in English class called "If They Chop Open My Body." It was all about what they'd find inside the author if anyone dared to do such a thing. Some of the things were silly, like a silver Suburban with the keys in it still idling in her rib cage. But our teacher said it was *metaphorical,* and I sort of understood because of the bit that said when they chopped her open they also found a little girl in a magenta pinafore saying over and over, "I'm getting tired of walking." A pinafore is an apron, apparently.

One line said if they chopped her open they would find that all along a woman named Rita had been inside her doing the cha-cha in turquoise beads and a swishy black dress. I had nightmares that I was being chopped open so that people could find the money and buy booze with it. It didn't feel like a metaphor, it felt real.

Someone from the newspaper kept calling and calling, asking to interview me. Dumpling's father said "No interviews" in that firm but nice way he talks. My mom and her friends had been coming around more often; Dumpling's dad would sit out on the porch and chat with them, and when Mom asked about me he'd just say, "Dora's doing real fine."

There is nothing at all scary about Paula and Annette—or my mom, for that matter—unless you count the way they like to drink and how they avert their eyes from bad things happening right under their own roof. I would give them all my winnings if I thought it would change things, but even I'm not that dumb.

Besides, the way the Ice Classic works is that the money goes directly into the bank, so nobody can get it. I'm not even sure how to get it myself.

"Do you know how a bank account works?" I ask Dumpling.

"I think you just walk in with your account number and

school ID and tell them what you want," she says, but I know she doesn't know, either. Her mother wraps dollar bills in foil and stores them in the freezer in case the house burns down.

I imagine a pretty bank teller with gobs of hair spray looking at my picture, smiling at me, and saying, "How much money would you like, Dora Peters?" It seems too easy, like a movie or a dream or someone else's life. Dumpling's dad said he'd go down with me and we could put it into an account where it wouldn't be allowed to be touched until I was eighteen.

I'm thinking about that, but there is a part of me that thinks it might be nice to have some money. So far, it seems safe.

After almost a month the newspaper stopped bugging me, and then my mom and her friends stopped dropping by, so I figured maybe everybody had forgotten that I'd won, which shows how a person can get soft living with a family like Dumpling's.

I also got sidetracked watching Ruth Lawrence get on a bus one night all by herself. She had a small brown suitcase and a ratty red coat, and from Dumpling's upstairs window I saw her sitting on the merry-go-round, waiting for the bus. It wasn't the suitcase or the way she obviously looked like she was leaving or running away that shocked me, but that Dumpling was sitting with her. When had they started doing that?

It made me dizzy watching them, as if I were the one

spinning around and around, because I should have been. We had rules in Birch Park, and those rules did not include Ruth and Dumpling sitting together, talking like friends, keeping secrets from me, like the scrap of blue paper that Ruth gave to Dumpling. I'll admit that I was more than happy to see Ruth get on the bus with its Yukon license plate and squeaky brakes, so loud that you'd think someone inside the Lawrence house would have come out to see—or say good-bye. A curtain fluttered in their kitchen window, but that was all. Not even Lily?

Inside the bus, Ruth just stared out the window straight ahead as if there was nothing she wanted more than for that bus to shift into gear and take her away, too.

After the bus pulled out, Dumpling's dad went outside and sat down on the merry-go-round next to Dumpling, his bulky frame out of place where only us kids usually ever sit. I wanted to know what they were saying and how Dumpling could possibly be friends with Ruth, and why she'd never even told me. Her father put his arm around Dumpling, as if something about Ruth Lawrence leaving could make them sad, or had anything to do with them.

It hit me like a meteorite: I'm not really part of this family, no matter how nice they are to me. It's possible that someday they might send me back.

The next morning I watched Dumpling as she braided her hair. I waited for her to tell me what she and Ruth were doing on the merry-go-round and what Ruth had given her—there had to be a good explanation. She pulled a red ribbon out of her cigar box, and I saw the blue note, tucked into the pile of ribbons as if guarded by a bunch of fraying red snakes. But Dumpling just shut the lid without even mentioning it.

"That Ruth Lawrence is sure getting pudgy," I said.

Dumpling tied the ribbon to the end of her braid without saying anything.

Normally I am unflappable, like a still, still pond without one single ripple. I have had years of practice. But like I said, living with Dumpling's family has softened me around the edges. I have started to let my guard down and not just wait for someone to beat the living daylights out of me. It's not the big things that are undoing me anymore, but something as simple as Dumpling having a silly secret involving Ruth Lawrence. It feels like my best friend has just skipped a pebble across the glassy surface of my soul.

If you chopped open my body, you'd see every jealous little wave as it slapped against my sternum.

She didn't look at me as she ran her finger over the fake Indian on her cigar box.

"Her dad and my dad were really good friends," she said. "They worked together on native rights, trying to protect our land and stuff."

I stared at the ridiculous headdress and the long black braids of the cigar Indian. I've never seen an Indian that looked like that. And I've never thought about Lily and Ruth having parents, either; they've always just lived with their gran.

"Her dad died in a plane crash," Dumpling said. "My dad told me to try to understand how that might feel."

I know what it would feel like if my dad died in a plane crash—great. But I didn't say that. I didn't say anything, because Dumpling having anything in common with Ruth had left me totally speechless.

Summer kept us out later and later, just spinning on the merry-go-round and talking about the money I won, which still just felt like Monopoly money. We made a game of imagining all the things I could buy with it.

"You could buy some new boots from Sears Roebuck next winter," Dumpling said.

"And socks that aren't worn thin on the bottoms from someone else wearing them first," I added.

"Yeah," she said wistfully, like she'd never thought of that before.

"What would *you* buy?" I asked her.

"Maybe a new outboard for my dad? He needs a bigger horsepower engine; the old one kept dying last summer at fish camp," she said. "Or a new cookstove for my mom."

But I had too many things on my own list to think about others: boots, socks, big metal locks on all the doors, and if there was a way to buy Dumpling's family permanently as my own and never have to leave, I'd happily use all the money for that.

When the reporter drove up in a brown-paneled station wagon, Dumpling and I weren't paying that much attention.

I certainly wasn't expecting them to still care about the Ice Classic—we were well into summer now.

I realized right away that it was Selma's mom, because Selma was sitting in the front seat. Her mom got out and walked over to where we sat spinning around lazily, but Selma stayed put, breathing onto the window and then drawing little doodles on it. It was immediately obvious that Selma really is adopted, just like she's always bragged.

Selma isn't fat, but she's doughy, and she has thick ankles and a round face, while her mother is all pointy and angular, as if she was built by students in a remedial geometry class. She stuck out her hand, which looked like fanned-out twigs on the end of a skinny branch, and said to Dumpling, "Hi, I'm Abigail Flowers. You must be Dora." Apparently Dumpling looks like someone who would win a big wad of money and I do not.

Dumpling just smiled and tilted her head in my direction.

"Oh," she said. "Sorry. Hi, Dora, Abigail." I shook the tips of her twiggy fingers.

"So, do you feel like talking about winning the Ice Classic yet? People would still like to hear your version of things. It would be a great 'feel-good' story. A nice change from always reading bad news, you know?"

She flipped open her skinny reporter notepad that looked just like her and licked the tip of a pencil.

No, I didn't know. A change from reading bad news in general, or just bad news about us? I still cringed at the way the paper had called me the first "native" girl to win the jackpot. Why didn't they just say the youngest and leave it at that? Now she wanted me to be the poster child for a "feel-good" story? I would have laughed if it had been even the tiniest bit funny.

I looked over at Selma sitting in the car and wondered what it's like to live in a house where people ask what you're thinking and how you feel. Is that why Selma blabs all the time about her life?

I was glad she stayed in the car, but then I realized the real reason she hadn't gotten out was because Ruth was the only reason Selma ever came here in the first place. If Dumpling knows where Ruth went, she has never said anything. Lily said Ruth went to visit family in Canada, but that's a load of crap. Everyone knows what's going on with Ruth, except maybe her own sister, because if her gran said that Ruth was now living on the moon, Lily and probably Bunny would believe that, too.

When Selma's mom asked me to describe how I felt about winning the Ice Classic, how I felt was that it was none of her goddamn business. If she chopped open my body, she might have been surprised that there were no dollar bills hanging off my clavicle or flapping from my rib cage.

In the end, though, I said nothing, because the interview was interrupted by a white van flying into the parking lot, tires screeching and dust blowing everywhere. Its bumper hung at a crooked angle—like a half-smile on a drunk man— and I knew before the door even opened who was going to fall out of that van. And then he did, still in an orange jumpsuit, fresh from the Fairbanks Correctional Center. I knew he'd get out of jail sometime, and of course it had to be right then, because it is *my life*, after all.

Dumpling looked horrified. Abigail Flowers looked surprised. From inside the fogged-up car, Selma just looked scared.

"Dora, you get over here!" he yelled, stopping a few feet from us and looking at the notebook in Selma's mom's hand. I saw a flicker of recognition dart across her face. She was most likely the reporter who did the story on my dad shooting up the Sno-Go, too. It's not like Fairbanks has a million reporters. She must know everything about everyone. Was this what she meant about doing a "feel-good" story? Yeah, there's a twist: *the girl whose father shot up the Sno-Go just happened to win the Ice Classic.*

"Mr. Peters," she said, and instantly I knew she'd gone too far. She'd meant to sound polite, but his lip curled at the word *Mr.* as if she was mocking him.

"You don't want to break your parole in the first hour you're out now, do you?"

"Get away from my daughter!" he shouted.

But instead of stepping away, like a sane person, she actually turned and put herself between me and my dad; Dumpling, too, as if her bony frame could protect us all.

Selma's terrified eyes were wide and unblinking in the front seat of the car.

"Don't make me call the police," Abigail said.

"No, it's okay." I tried to step around her. You'd think a reporter would at least know the rules. If she called the police, things would get even worse for me than they already were.

"That's right, Dora. Whaddya think? That you'd get to keep all that money for yerself?" he said.

Out of the corner of my eye, I saw Dumpling's father coming out of their house. He made a beeline straight toward my dad, his hand extended in greeting, as if he were actually glad to see him.

"Welcome back, Bumpo; let's go have a chat down at the diner."

"If that little slut daughter of mine thinks she's hoarding that money . . ."

Dumpling's dad winced at the word *slut,* but he put his arm around my father as if they were old pals and said, "Let's discuss it with the brothers."

Hills Bros. coffee is just called "the brothers" around here. But I'm sure my dad would've preferred something stiffer. He must've been pretty thirsty if he really did just get out of jail.

Behind his back, Dumpling's father motioned with his hand that Dumpling and I should go inside the house. Nobody had to tell me twice.

We leave for Dumpling's fish camp that very night when Dumpling's father gets back. Nobody asks him where my dad is or what happened; we just load everything into their station wagon and drive through the bright reddish-orange night, up past the White Mountains and to the edge of the mighty Yukon River.

Nobody says one word about my dad or the white van or Selma's mom asking me questions. We drive farther and farther north, the single-lane road dipping like a roller coaster where beneath it the ground has frozen and thawed—like it does every year—ripping apart asphalt that needs to be redone every single summer.

I breathe easier with each green mile marker we pass on the side of the road. For most people, these numbers just mark the location of someone's cabin, or gold mine, or a spot where they once shot a moose. But for me it means putting more and more distance between me and my dad.

We drive for hours to the banks of the Yukon, then unload everything into the boat that Dumpling's dad leaves here every fall—pulling off the not-so-white tarp and shaking off the debris that's built up over the year. A lot of boats are already gone from their winter spots, as people head upriver like the salmon themselves.

Up and down the Yukon, fish wheels punctuate the river looking like miniature carnival rides, with long-handled scoops made of chicken wire, turned by the river's current. Dumpling has told me that there is nothing more exciting than reaching inside the fish box and lifting a salmon out by its mouth.

Dumpling's dad fiddles with the outboard, and her mom gives us all pilot bread smeared with peanut butter. It's two a.m. but we are wide-awake, skipping rocks under the midnight sun, giddy about getting the boat in the water. I remember Dumpling saying her dad needed a bigger horsepower engine for this skiff and I hope it will still make it up the river, especially with an extra person on board.

Dumpling looks at me as if she's reading my mind.

"He can make this thing run with nothing but duct tape and bear grease, don't worry," she says.

Dumpling and Bunny sit on five-gallon gas cans, but since I am the guest, they let me lay across the gear—garbage bags full of blankets and coats and lumpier cargo like pots and pans and a cast-iron skillet. They laugh when I suddenly say "Ouch!" and feel underneath me, pulling out the ax we brought to chop firewood.

I gaze up at the peregrine falcons nesting high on the cliffs as we motor north. The memory of my dad grows smaller and smaller, darting in and out of my brain like the tiny black dots flying above me. It's hours and hours until we get upriver, and I sleep through them all—more hours than I have slept at one stretch in years.

The engine dying down wakes me in time to see Dumpling step a rubber boot gingerly into the shallow water and pull the boat forward, tying us to a ruddy spruce tree. Dumpling's mother immediately climbs the bank, looking like a bushy-tailed squirrel pulling brush and downed limbs together to get a fire going.

Bunny is trying to unload the garbage bags I've been sleeping on, yanking at them and pushing me off; we roll around wrestling in the bottom of the boat until Dumpling starts rocking it back and forth, threatening to flip us over. Life feels light and easy now, laughing with Bunny and being far away from Fairbanks.

Suddenly everyone is bustling around, sweeping mouse and rabbit turds off the wooden tent platform, chopping wood and putting tents up on poles, stringing together the racks for drying fish, and getting the charred black coffeepot full of the brothers brewing on the fire. Everything has a purpose here, even me.

My parents have never bothered about stocking up salmon for the winter. Dumpling's father has always been generous, bringing fish back for everyone at Birch Park, so my mom would just shrug and say, "Why work so hard?" whenever the subject came up. But it doesn't feel like work.

It feels like being part of a family.

CHAPTER SEVEN

Don't Ask, Don't Tell

ALYCE

The day the ferry passed us, I was the only person who saw the boy fall overboard into the pod of orcas. The ferry made no attempt to turn around; nobody on deck seemed to notice him. I had never launched the *Pelican* all by myself before, but adrenaline is a remarkable thing.

Then again, so is sheer luck. Dad was busy talking on the radio (it takes all his concentration) and Uncle Gorky was down in the engine room, which is why they never even saw me struggling to untie and move the *Pelican* from the flying bridge to the deck and then into the water. There just wasn't time to think or talk or ask permission. By the time they finally saw me, I was rowing my inflatable raft straight into the whales. I have no idea what they must have been thinking. I do know what I was thinking: *Please, please, please don't let me be too late.*

But then he appeared on the surface, a boy about my age, though it was really hard to tell from that angle. He was floating facedown and I was able to grab one arm of his waterlogged plaid coat. He wasn't wearing a life jacket, so it was odd that he was on the surface, especially since he was unconscious. Or was he dead? Maybe I really was too late. That's when I started wishing I'd at least brought Uncle Gorky.

I tugged, but he was so heavy that surely I could not pull this body into my boat, and I was becoming more and more panicked with every minute that went by. "Come on, you lug," I said to him, as if insults might do the trick, and all of a sudden not only the arm but the whole body was suddenly light. I fell backward into the *Pelican* and the boy landed right beside me as if he'd jumped in all on his own. But he wasn't moving at all. A loud bark and then a clicking noise next to the raft got my attention. I looked over to see the oily black nose of a whale, so close I could smell his breath.

"Were you the one helping me?" I whispered. Underneath my hand the cool, smooth nose felt like butter. I was so mesmerized I almost forgot about the unconscious body in my raft, until the orca nudged the side of the *Pelican,* turning me back to face the *Squid,* which was headed toward us. This boy really was about my age—I could see this now, his wet hair flat against his skull. His features were chiseled like a Roman sea god, and he looked peaceful, not like someone who had been struggling to get out of the ocean. I had heard a lot of gruesome stories about bodies that wash up, but this one was not gruesome by any stretch. He was not pale or colorless, or cut up or bloody. And I'm only going to say this once, because it shocked me—both that he looked this way and that I thought it in the midst of panicking and rowing and being so close to an orca—but this boy was beautiful.

I dipped my oars and the orca pushed the side of the *Pelican* one more time, hard enough that I heard the rubber of the raft squeak beneath his smooth nose, and then the huge whale dipped his body back under the surface. I was able to see the gray patch on his back—the saddle—and wondered what it would be like to ride him, even as I knew I was wasting valuable time. I began to row hard.

I was still running on adrenaline, but my dad was visibly shaken as he and Uncle Gorky hauled the unconscious boy onto the *Squid*. He tied the *Pelican* so loosely to the stern that I had to retie or she'd have floated away.

I watched him pressing on the boy's chest and breathing into his mouth, and the whole time I could not stop thinking about the way the orca seemed to be helping me, pushing the boy up out of the ocean and into the raft. Looking at him sprawled across the deck, I wondered if he might actually die. His long legs were bent beneath him; his feet were bare except for one red sock on the left one. No shoes.

Finally he began to gag and throw up kelp onto the deck, belching seaweed and salt water until the whole ocean seemed to come out of him. Inside my own chest, that hard knot of fear that he was dead floated free as I watched him choke and painfully draw in air. And then we were both able to breathe again. After a while Uncle Gorky carried him to the big bunk, where he's been for two days now.

My uncle keeps telling me to let him sleep. "Leave him be, Alyce," he says, but I want to be there when he opens his eyes. I can't get out of my head the image of that one orca staring at me with his wide black eye, as if he was telling me something. It's not the kind of thing you tell Uncle Gorky. "The orca and I have an understanding and I need to look into this boy's eyes when he wakes up. It was kind of like a promise."

Yeah, right. I have those kinds of conversations all the time with my dad and my uncle.

But when he does finally wake, it's obvious that he is not happy or grateful or any of the scenarios I played out in my mind. If anything, he looks disappointed. I feel embarrassed to be propped so close to his face, my chin on the edge of the bunk.

"Where are the orcas?" is all he asks, but his voice still sounds like it's underwater and I can tell it burns him to use it. When he coughs it sounds exactly how the orcas sounded that day they woke me up on the flying bridge. Maybe he didn't want to be rescued after all? He keeps a wall up between himself and the rest of us that feels impenetrable. Asking anything seems rude. So far all he'll let me do is tilt his head up so he can take small sips of water. I smell the sea in his hair. But then he lies back down and closes his eyes. It's clear he wants to be left alone.

Later my dad takes him a mug of tea, and I sit on the open hatch of the fo'c'sle, eavesdropping despite Uncle Gorky's disapproving look. Dad sloshes the tea on the way down the ladder, and I hear him say, "Shit," in that way that always makes me laugh because it's so lacking in real emotion—why even bother? It reminds me of Mom complaining that Dad is an "underreactor," like that's a bad thing. If I lie on my belly, I can look down into the fo'c'sle and just barely see them. Dad props up the boy's head and holds the mug to his lips, saying, "Careful, this is dangerous," as if swimming in the ocean is nothing compared to the riskier task of drinking tea on a boat.

"You want to talk?" he asks.

The boy shakes his head.

"Didn't think so," he says.

I can tell this conversation is going nowhere.

"I'm George," Dad says, and then turns to head back up the ladder.

"Sam," says the boy. "I'm Sam." I see my dad look back at him and nod. Then he pauses and decides it's okay to mention one more thing.

"I did check with the Marine Highway, and they say they aren't missing any passengers."

Sam just stares at my ballet slippers hanging on the nail, and I feel my cheeks grow warm.

"You just rest," Dad says. "If there's no rush getting you back, it would be great if we could finish up the king opening. There's still another week and a half and I can't afford not to fish. That okay with you?"

Sam nods.

I didn't know my dad checked in with the ferry, and I can't stop asking him and Uncle Gorky why they aren't more curious that there was no record of Sam. I know he was on that boat; I saw him.

Dad says more words than usual when he tells me in no uncertain terms that he doesn't stick his nose in where it doesn't belong. I'm beginning to see my mom's point about Dad being an underreactor. We rescued a boy in the ocean and he's just going to keep fishing?

"You haven't learned the way of the sea yet, Alyce?" Uncle Gorky says to me. "Don't ask, don't tell."

"But he's my age," I say.

"Doesn't matter. If somebody tried to unravel the secrets in this ocean, there would be no age limit. And it would be like opening Pandora's box, if you ask me. If this boat ever goes down, you think those ballet slippers hanging there wouldn't be a mystery to somebody?"

Uncle Gorky always knows how to shut me up. I do not want to talk about my ballet slippers.

Sam being on the *Squid* has certainly taken my mind off dancing, though. After a few more days, he finally comes out on deck to look around. He looks so pale and thin, I don't think Dad wants to make him do anything. But slowly he asks me about how things work on the boat. I feel like I'm reading an inventory list of the gear.

"This is a cleaning tray," I say, slicing through the neck bone of a king salmon and making him wince. I was actually trying to impress him.

"Sorry," I say. "It's only brutal the first time. Or maybe you've fished before?"

He shakes his head.

"My dad used to," he says.

But then he stops and I feel the invisible wall go up. *Okay, don't ask about a dad.*

"Are you ever going to tell me what you were doing on the ferry?" I try to sound as if I'm not actually prying.

He sighs.

"My brothers and I stowed away."

"Really?" Now I am impressed.

"Please don't tell your dad," he says. "I think my older brother could get arrested if they find them."

"But we should get them word that you're okay, don't you think?"

"I figure Hank probably saw you rescue me and knows I'm okay. He's just trying to figure out a way to get in touch without the authorities finding out. And he's probably really mad at me."

"Wouldn't he just be worried?"

"Not Hank. He acts like he's our dad now, and I'm always messing everything up. He's big on being in charge."

He won't look me in the eye. "I'm sure he knows I'm fine; he's just got to figure out how to get in touch."

This seems like a long shot, but I have more questions.

"Why did you run away in the first place?"

"Why are you so nosy?"

"I'm just curious," I say, feeling slapped. "I did save you, you know."

"Thanks," he mumbles, not at all grateful. I could tell him that I didn't see anyone else on the deck of the ferry and I doubt his brother knows he's safe. But if he thinks I'm too nosy, fine. I'll keep it to myself.

Slowly Sam starts doing small jobs like handing fish to Uncle Gorky down in the fish hold or hosing off the deck at the end of the day. Dad shows him how the trolling poles work, explaining that the little bells attached at the top will ring if there's a big fish on the hook. I don't know when I learned any of this. Maybe never, because I was born on the boat, so all of this stuff was just part of being human, like learning to talk and walk and breathe.

The moment Dad started seeing Sam as another pair of hands was probably the day the wind kicked up out of nowhere and Sam ran over to the stabilizer propped on the deck, undid the chain, and threw the whole thing overboard like he'd been doing it forever. Stabilizers are heavy weights on chains that are a pain to haul back in, so Dad avoids using them until it's so choppy we're flopping around like a tiny toy in a very large bathtub. I watch Dad watching Sam, starting to see him as someone who could eventually pull his own weight, skinny as he is.

* * *

The days start to bleed together one after another, and Sam and I fall into a routine of sitting on the flying bridge at the end of the day. Sometimes he even forgets to put up his impenetrable wall, and I get to learn a few more things about him. He's sixteen and likes poetry. His younger brother, Jack, is fourteen and has what Sam calls a "sixth sense."

"Sometimes it's weird," he says, "like he can feel things that other people can't."

I can tell he's thinking about his brothers a lot, but I don't ask direct questions anymore since he called me nosy, and I do keep my promise not to tell Dad.

I also finally tell him how the *Pelican* saved his life. He touches the rubber side of the inflatable raft, and I'm grateful he doesn't laugh when I say she was his rescuer. But I don't see her the same way I used to, either. She looks like nothing but an old beat-up raft, especially now that Sam is sitting next to her. I look at the duct-tape patches and the faded rubber that is almost white in spots from being bleached by the sun or the ocean or the passage of time. "Was there anyone else there?" he asks. "I mean, besides the whales?"

I think about the way the orca looked at me; how it blinked as if we had an understanding. But I still don't know how much I should say to this boy who is starting to make me feel weak in the knees. I tell myself it's just my sea legs, but I think Uncle Gorky would disagree. I've seen the way he looks at us, like we are a puzzle to be figured out. I don't see how anyone will figure out Sam, because if he is a puzzle, there are some big missing pieces that he isn't in any hurry to tell us about.

"No, just the whales," I say, and he looks disappointed. It's kind of the truth, but not the whole truth. I'm afraid I'll sound dumb, and I don't want him to stop talking to me again.

On the way back down, we stop on the bow, where Dad and Uncle Gorky's voices filter up through the open porthole. They must have forgotten it was open, because we can hear them talking about Sam.

"Are you going to tell him?" Uncle Gorky asks.

"I don't see how that's going to help now," says Dad.

"You should at least tell him you know who he is."

"And then what? Make him go back when obviously they were running away from something?"

"What about his brothers?"

"My guess is they were all on that ferry, probably stowaways. They'd have gotten off by now, even if they made it all the way to Seattle."

"You owe it to Martin."

I have no idea who Martin is, but Sam does. The color drains from his cheeks. He flies into the wheelhouse and I follow close behind him.

"You know my dad?" he says, making both Dad and Uncle Gorky jump and slosh their tea. "My dad's name is Martin; do you know him?"

Dad sets down his mug and stands up. "Sam, I knew your dad. And I know he was killed in the tsunami."

"NO!" Sam is shouting. "He's not dead, he's not dead. He's swimming with the orcas."

He sounds like a little kid, not a sixteen-year-old boy, and I would be embarrassed for him if I hadn't seen the way the orca had helped him, or felt the way I had when I touched that cold black nose. The minute Sam says those ridiculous words, I get it. The way he looked at me when he woke up; his disappointment at being rescued. Sam slumps onto the floor, the way you do when you've lost all hope and can never, ever go back.

Dad and Uncle Gorky look down at the oil marks soaked into the galley floor and out the window at the silent sea—anywhere but at Sam. I don't know how long they plan to leave him there—maybe forever—but I can't stand it.

I sit on the floor and wrap my arms around him while he buries his head in my shoulder and soaks me with his snot and tears. "I should probably find my brothers," he finally says to my dad, as if the memory of them is an orange life ring—something tangible to hold on to in the midst of a storm.

Without looking away from the ocean, my dad just dips his head in acknowledgment and says, "We'll find them."

Later Sam and I are down in the fo'c'sle, and even though it's pitch dark, I can tell he's not asleep. I let him keep the big bunk because it seemed childish to ask for it back, so I'm in the hammock that was my bed when I was much smaller. It's like sleeping in a mummy bag with my arms pinned to my sides.

"Sam?" I whisper.

"Hmm?"

"You know how you asked me about the whales? Well"—I pause—"I'm pretty sure the orca helped me save you."

I can just barely hear him breathing.

"I thought so at first, too," he says, "like he was telling me to kick off my shoes and swim with him. I felt like he was taking care of me."

"Maybe he was." I am thinking about the orca's smooth nose and his eye as big and round as a giant gumball.

"I don't think so," Sam says, as if he's suddenly aged a hundred years. "But thanks for not laughing."

"You didn't have any shoes on," I tell him, as if this proves something, but he's already shut the door on that thought. He doesn't respond and I hear him turn over in the big bunk, something that is nearly impossible in my tiny hammock.

I fall asleep and dream I am a hermit crab, living squished in the toe of a brown boot at the bottom of the deep blue sea.

CHAPTER EIGHT

On Being Noticed

HANK

Remember when my mother said *"You wait until your whole world falls out from under you"*? It turns out the world has many bottoms.

For the next two days, Jack and I somehow make our way around the *Matanuska* without Sam, but we still look for him behind every corner. As minutes turn into hours, the reality that Sam is really not on this boat burns in my chest, scarring my heart and my lungs until it's hard to take a deep breath. We find his jacket in one of the lifeboats on the side of the ferry, flapping in the wind like a detached brown wing. Now Jack sleeps with it every night, burying his face in the rough corduroy as if it has all the answers. He breathes in Sam's smell, believing in that Jack way that Sam will still be found, that he's out there somewhere, alive.

The only person who might have seen where Sam went got off the boat two stops back at some small port in Southeast, the rain torrential. The chicken lady hobbled down the metal off-ramp, an orange-clad ferry worker on each of her elbows, her wild hair whipping them in the face until the rain tamed it enough to sit flat against her skull. She looked like an injured bird herself, watching them load her precious chicken crate into an old Toyota truck. I could tell she wanted her chickens to go inside the cab, out of the weather. A young woman and a man got out and wrapped themselves around her, ignoring that she was wearing a garbage bag for a raincoat.

Maybe the man who picked her up was her son, shaking hands with the car deck crew like they were old friends, but I know from listening to whispered conversation that she was listed as a missing persons case. I overheard it when Jack and I were hiding in a life raft nearby, using puffy orange life jackets as pillows. She was supposed to be in a home for the mentally ill, but somehow she just walked away without anyone noticing. Jack was torn up about that part— that nobody even noticed. And he was pretty upset when I told him we had to distance ourselves from her, so as not to be connected with a missing person. But as she got into the blue truck, I whispered, "What did you see? Did he really fall overboard?" The door slammed shut behind her, and in that instant all hope of knowing what really happened was wrung out of me like water from a washrag.

Things between me and Jack have been tense since then.

"I had a dream about Sam," he tells me. I ignore him.

"It was a bouncy dream, with a boat and some whales."

I say nothing.

"It smelled like tea and flowers," he continues.

"Flowers are bad luck on boats," I say.

"Well, it smelled good, like lilacs."

I don't respond.

"Maybe we should think about going back," he says hesitantly. "In case Sam is looking for us."

His incessant optimism grates on me. I used to think it was sweet, but now it just reminds me of everything we've lost, and I can barely hold it together. "He's gone, Jack, so just knock it off."

He wraps the empty brown arms of Sam's jacket around himself like a hug and says nothing. I've lost one brother, and the other one is dissolving right in front of me. Even though I'm afraid I will lose him, too, I can't seem to stop it from happening. I don't know how to make a new plan, not knowing where Sam is. With no good plan, I just stay the course, which I know frustrates Jack.

He thinks I don't see his little private connection with the night watchman, either. But I do. When the watchman makes his rounds, the big, fat key ring jangles against the leg of his blue trousers, and I feel Jack's body alert like a cat. They make eye contact and I wonder what Jack is doing. There is part of me that wants to wave a white flag and surrender, retire from being "the man of the family," because I've done such a lousy job of it anyway. But even that would take energy, and I only have enough left to keep moving every couple hours, changing spots every time the memory of Sam catches up with me.

We have slept like french fries under heat lamps in the solarium, in the life rafts with the life jackets as pillows, under the stairwell near the car deck, and now in the little play area with the humongous plastic Legos, which is deserted because it's three a.m. Parents have been known to leave their kids here and go off to the bar. At least, that's what you believe if you listen to the announcements that come over the loudspeaker at least twice a day. "Will the parents of a four-year-old girl wearing a Mickey Mouse jean jacket please return to the play area on the second level."

For now we're the only ones here, sleeping on thick blue mats under a sign that says DO NOT LEAVE CHILDREN UNATTENDED IN THE PLAY AREA.

The night watchman has a clicker in his hand that I've grown accustomed to. He must have to click when he's inspected a part of the ship—some sort of log—so I have heard his clicks from almost every spot on the boat. I can feel Jack relax, as if the clicker is comforting. He seems worried that maybe, like the chicken lady, nobody has even noticed we're gone. Not even the people we were trying to get away from. I imagine he hears the night watchman's footsteps and then *click, click,* someone has noticed us, two boys alone; *click, click,* someone sees us; *click,* someone cares; *click,* someone is turning out the lights for us. *Click, click.*

*   *   *

When I wake up alone in the play area, my first thought is that Jack has done a Sam—*poof*. Gone.

By the time I find Jack in the dining car playing cribbage with the night watchman, I'm too relieved to say anything. The cribbage board has ivory pegs made from walrus tusks—exactly like the one my father had. If he hadn't left, maybe Sam would still be here, too.

It's too hard trying to keep track of brothers who are full of their own ideas. They're like helium balloons. At some point you just have to let go of the string and say, "Go on, then—good-bye, safe travels," which has got to be easier than wondering whether you're going to hold on too tight and pop the damn thing. Is that what happened to Sam?

I sit down across from the cribbage board. Jack won't quite meet my eye.

"Have you learned to count your own points, then?" I ask, trying to sound casual, but my heart is still back in the play area, beating like a terrified rabbit.

"He's never been able to quite get the hang of the points," I say to the night watchman, when Jack doesn't answer.

"He holds his own pretty well," the man says.

His face is lined like a map; he's worked outside on boats for so many years it's creased in all the right places.

He smiles and holds out a wide, weathered hand for me to shake. "I'm Phil," he says.

Then he goes back to the game.

Jack holds his cards in front of his face, as if he's trying to make himself disappear. How long exactly has he been sneaking off, playing cribbage with Phil?

"Is that it, then?" I ask. "Are we in trouble?"

I'm so tired, if Jack wants to turn us in, then let's get it over with so I can lie down and sleep right here under this booth. I just want to curl up with the scattered cold fries, empty wrappers, and smell of rubber boots and go to sleep for a million years.

Phil lays down a card, moves a peg, and does not look at me.

"Years ago I was the harbormaster in a little fishing town," he says conversationally. "One night I went into the harbor bathroom and there was a brand-new little baby. Couldn't have been more than a couple days old at most. She still had her little shrunken umbilical cord sticking out of her belly button; it hadn't even fallen off. She was practically blue, naked, just lying in the stainless steel sink."

Jack looks at me and raises an eyebrow, but I wonder where he's going with this odd story.

"I wrapped her in paper towels and my raincoat—which wasn't nearly warm enough—but she was so cold and I was just worried she might not make it; I guess I went on autopilot," he says. "Maybe I was in shock or something. It's not like you ever expect to find something like that."

"Your turn," he says to Jack, as if this is totally normal chitchat to have in the middle of a cribbage game.

"What happened?" I whisper, afraid that he's going to tell us the baby died.

"Long story short, she was tough as nails and perked up pretty fast once I got her warm. There was, of course, a bunch of news attention and a search for who had left her, but no one ever turned up. She did wind up in a really nice family, moved up north," he says. "She's about your age now"—he nods at me—"maybe a little younger. She survived me being the first on the scene and knowing nothing about babies, and the scratchy woolen blanket that I finally found for her, *and* being abandoned. She was a little fireball."

He looks at his watch. "I have to go make my rounds," he tells Jack, "so we can just hold this hand if you want. No cheating while I'm gone."

"Do you know her still?" Jack asks, and Phil sits back down.

"I lost touch," he says, a note of sadness in his voice. "For her sake," he adds, "in case she didn't want to be reminded of the worst thing that ever happened to her."

"Maybe you were the best thing that ever happened to her," Jack says, unable to *not* be himself. But his optimism stabs me in the chest, reminding me again that Sam is gone.

"What about us?" I can't help it. I'm so tired of running and hiding and being in charge. I think about curling myself into a semicircle and sleeping on this bench until the police come to take us back home. Surely that's what will happen, even as I hear myself say, "We can't go home." My voice sounds flat, like a tire worn down to the rim.

"It's funny," Phil says, as if to himself. "I took this job because every time I walked by that bathroom in the harbor, I was afraid of what I might find. It was fine; I mean, it could have been way worse. If she hadn't been alive I don't know what I would have done. But it still made me nervous; I didn't want any more surprises on the job."

"At least we have our clothes on," Jack says, which makes Phil laugh so deep and loud, I'm sure he's going to wake up the entire ferry.

"You guys aren't so bad," he says, "but I wonder what it is with me and stray kids."

I follow the creases on Phil's face. Maybe the lines really are a map.

"You two need to decide what you want to do and then let me know how I can help, within the bounds of the law," he says, wiping his eyes from laughing so hard.

Then he stands up again to go make his rounds, but before he leaves he lays down a brown paper towel with writing on it that I recognize as Jack's.

In big, blocky letters it says: CAN YOU HELP US? WE NEED TO GET BACK TO FIND MY BROTHER. PLEASE DON'T TURN US IN. WE ARE DESPRATE.

Now it's my turn to laugh, rocking back and forth until my gut hurts. Jack stares at me. But I can't help it. When I'm finally able to catch my breath, I say, "We're *desprate*? Jack, you really should have tried harder in spelling."

Phil turns out to be an okay guy who doesn't turn us in to the ship's captain, which surprises me. In fact, I am more resigned now that Phil knows our secret, and I even let Jack choose the fake names we've decided to use. When he says I'll be called Oscar and he'll be Frank, I wonder if that was a mistake. Especially because every time he says "Oscar," he starts humming the Oscar Mayer wiener song. Laughing was something I'd never thought I'd do again, not as Hank or Oscar or anyone, and I'm amazed how much it helps. Although without Sam, I know the darkness is always close by.

I don't tell Jack that I'm grateful he turned us in, but I do feel about a thousand pounds lighter now that Phil is helping us. He says a friend of his knows a family in Fairbanks willing to take us in until I turn eighteen.

Phil warned me, though, that if I try to run off alone and we get caught again, we could get separated. The state might not care so much about me living on my own, but Jack's still young enough to raise eyebrows.

"I hear you, Phil. I promise, no more running."

It was enough to scare me into following the rules. Well, sort of. We still had to use fake names, because no way was I going to let Jack anywhere near Nathan Hodges again, either. I had a hunch that Phil knew those weren't our real names anyway.

In Prince Rupert Phil introduces us to Isabelle, the Canadian version of social services. She's wearing a plaid wool skirt and short little rain boots with dogwood and fireweed blooms painted on them, as if she's determined to blend into the scenery. Phil walks us up the ramp and gives her a hug that looks a tiny bit more than just professional, if you ask me. She turns to us and shakes our hands, much more formally. I've never known a woman who wore lipstick before, and this one has so much on she looks clownish. I can tell Jack is fighting the urge to laugh.

"Hello, Frank and Oscar," the bright-pink lips are saying. It takes me a minute to remember that we are Frank and Oscar. She opens the door of a rusty yellow Datsun that is supposed to make it all the way to Fairbanks. I'm a tad doubtful that this car will make the journey, but what choice do we have?

Just before we climb in, Phil puts his arms around our shoulders and pulls us both in close for a hug. "She's going to help you guys, I promise. She's also my girlfriend, so don't give her any trouble. She cut through a lot of red tape and is sticking her neck out here for all of us, so be nice."

Then he leans down close to look right into Jack's eyes. "I hope you find your brother," he says, slipping a square of brown paper towel into Jack's hand. "And just in case you're in her neck of the woods and you happen to run into her, say hello from me."

We wave good-bye from the back of the Datsun, and Jack unfolds the paper towel to find just one word written on it. In large letters scrawled in black marker, it says SELMA.

CHAPTER NINE

The Snowball Effect

RUTH

I finally did hear Gran talking to someone, the night I left home clutching my suitcase and the bus ticket to Canada. This time she was the one with the long red phone cord stretched into her room; through the door I thought I heard muffled crying. I couldn't really make out much. Just the words, "I'm sorry, Sister, I know. I didn't know what else to do." Gran sorry? And since when did she have a sister?

Before I went out to wait for the bus, she had said only that I didn't have to worry—she had made all the arrangements and that I wouldn't be alone. I searched her face, trying to figure out if I was being punished or if she really did think she was helping. I'm honestly not sure, but her face was softer than I'd ever seen it. She patted my shoulder and said, "Be good," and then mysteriously added, "Just try to understand."

But mostly I tried not to think about anything as the bus drove farther and farther into the Canadian Yukon. I was finally going to the place that had swallowed up my dad. It felt vast and empty except for trees and mountains and wide, open spaces. I doubted I would ever understand anything. After days of traveling on a very bumpy road that did no favors for my bladder, we pulled up to the abbey gates and I read the delightful sign, OUR LADY OF PERPETUAL SORROW. *Really, Gran? You have outdone yourself this time.*

That was already three weeks ago, but it feels like forever.

My belly is so round, I can put the white wicker clothes basket over it and pretend it's just a big ball of laundry. At this moment, instead of a baby, I could be pregnant with four flat sheets, two tea towels, and a pillowcase. Don't I wish.

My job here at the abbey is to take the laundry off the line for the Sisters. I say laundry, but there's only ever sheets and towels and sometimes my own clothes, because the nuns do their own washing and I doubt they own real clothes, but I don't know for sure. Living with Gran was good practice for not asking too many questions, even when a person is suddenly sent to a convent in another country and is the youngest person there by about seven hundred years.

I'm making a list of questions anyway, in case someone unexpectedly says to me, "So, Ruth, is there anything you'd like to know before your life goes any farther down this black hole?" In no particular order: *Are there ever any other girls like me who come here? Will the people who adopt my baby be kind? What will happen to me afterward? Does God hate me?*

Some days I take that last one off the list because I think the answer's probably obvious, but Sister Bernadette did tell me once that God only operates from a place of love. Then she hurried off really fast like she had something in her eye.

I haven't heard from anyone since I've been here. I didn't really expect to, but it makes it a million times lonelier and gives me a couple more questions for my list: *Are they even curious about where I am? Do Selma and Lily ever wonder about me? Does Dumpling still have my note?*

The flip side is that it's also kind of nice no one can see me, now that I'm the size of a house. I can't believe I still have months to go; how much bigger can I possibly get?

The nuns are all right, except for Sister Agnes, who I can tell is not happy that I'm here. Her face looks like a sprouted potato, but it's her personality that sticks with you. Gran would call it having "no front porch"—you can pretty much see straight into her mind, like looking into a cluttered living room, and it's obvious how she feels. I'd have known even if I hadn't overheard her talking to Sister Bernadette. They didn't know I was in the pantry, right off the kitchen where they were obviously arguing.

SISTER AGNES: I really thought Mother Superior had had enough of her nonsense by now.
SISTER BERNADETTE: Oh, Sister Agnes—how can you hold such a grudge after all this time?

SISTER AGNES: It's like an illness that just keeps getting passed on down the line in that family.

SISTER BERNADETTE: The abbess would disapprove of your assessment, Sister.

SISTER AGNES: The abbess did her best with Marguerite and obviously it had no effect.

SISTER BERNADETTE: OH, SISTER, HUSH.

SISTER AGNES: I can understand once, but three times? When is she going to put her foot down?

I was so confused that the name Marguerite went sailing right over my head. If the Sisters hadn't opened the pantry door at just that moment, I might have caught on sooner, but they found me sitting on a big bag of rice with a box of crackers in my hand, crumbs all down the front of me, and suddenly I had bigger fish to fry. (I get really hungry between meals.) Finding me in there only seemed to have proved some point that Sister Agnes was trying to make, because she looked at Sister Bernadette with an I-told-you-so expression.

Sister Bernadette and Sister Agnes are so ancient, they could easily be ghosts. But they bicker like sisters. I didn't realize nuns could be so human—holding grudges, arguing, making faces at each other and then storming away from disagreements like large winged bats. It's this unforeseen display of humanness that makes me feel better about them, like they're real people. Hearing them also makes me miss Lily in the most unexpected way.

I try to make sense of the strange conversation I heard in the pantry, but as the days go by, I have other pressing matters to think about. Such as my bladder now being the size of a walnut. I wake up almost every hour and waddle down the long, echoey corridor to the bathroom. All fourteen stations of the cross are lined up so that I walk by each one before I finally get there—the ripe smell of incense lingering in the hall, coming up through the vents and mingling with the sweet, honeyed scent of melted candle wax. Maybe I'm just dreaming and this isn't real. It's just a bad dream in which I'm trapped inside my old copy of *The Children's Illustrated Bible*. But it's a long walk with a full bladder, and it's definitely real.

There is Jesus, carrying his cross right beside me. We are quite the pair—he and I—but everyone knows what's in store for him at the end of that long walk, and I wouldn't put it past Gran to have sent me here solely to scare the living daylights out of me. Even after I'm back in bed, it's pretty hard to forget the images of the crown of thorns and the nails stuck in his hands and feet—the soldiers divvying up his clothes like vultures.

Catholics are pretty good at keeping Jesus nailed to that cross, rather than focusing more on that happy bit where he rose from the dead and freed us from sin and evil. It's like Gran not wanting us to feel too good about ourselves. As if that's a concern anymore. I'm not sure there will be any rising from anything after I'm done here. Unlike Jesus ascending into heaven, I feel like I'm just headed right over a cliff.

*   *   *

The nuns do a lot of different things to support themselves. They make soaps and lotions and have beehives that make honey and chickens that lay eggs. Sister Josephine takes everything to the mercantile in town once a week, and I get up my nerve to ask if I can go with her. Sister Bernadette frowns, like she thinks this is a very bad idea, but I tell her I've done all the laundry already and what harm can it do for me to go out into the world for just one day? She eyes my belly as if she's thinking that a person's life can actually change pretty dramatically in just one day, but then she looks away, as if nuns shouldn't be thinking things like that. Her face is slightly flushed when she says, "Okay, but just this once."

Sister Josephine is about half the age of Sister Agnes and Sister Bernadette, but that doesn't mean she's young. She's also the tallest nun I've ever seen—at least six feet, if not more. She has a row of whiskers on her upper lip and a few stray hairs popping out of her chin, which are very distracting to look at. She drives way too fast in the old green pickup, taking the corners at a clip that sends me flying across the cab. But it's the potholes I wish she'd slow down for. I am clutching my stomach with one hand and holding on to the dashboard for dear life with the other when she looks over and says, "Oh my goodness," as if she forgot I was here.

"I have a bit of a lead foot," she says apologetically, slowing down just a smidgen. "I grew up on a farm and started driving when I was ten, so it's kind of a thrill for me to get out on the road every week."

She's so much chattier than the other nuns, and I feel out of practice holding up my end of the conversation. "Mother Superior is so good about knowing what each one of us needs and which skills we have that will best serve. She handed me the keys to this old beauty the minute I was fully professed, which was quite an honor."

"What does it mean to be professed?" I ask.

"Oh, it's the very, very, very last stage, when you take your final vows. You have to go through a test period for six months, and then you become a novitiate for two years if you seem a good fit, and then you take temporary vows for no less than three years. And then you get professed, which is your final vows. So it's not a very spontaneous decision to commit yourself to this life."

I want to say it would have been nice if there were a similar process for getting pregnant, but that would come out wrong, so I don't. And then she surprises me by saying, "I would have thought your gran would have told you all this."

I'm more stunned than when she was flying over the potholes.

"You know my gran?"

Her wimple reminds me of the white folds on a turkey's neck as she swivels her head to look at me. "Of course; she grew up here at Our Lady, from when she was three years old. She really took me under her wing and showed me the ropes. She was such a fun, chatty teenager—not what you'd expect to find in a convent—she never told you about us?"

I shake my head, too shocked to say anything.

"Hmm, I wonder . . . ," she says. But she doesn't say what she wonders, and I'm still so stunned by Gran being fun and chatty that I don't notice we've pulled into the parking lot of a log cabin, which turns out to be the mercantile and the post office all rolled into one. Sister Josephine is already hopping out of the truck. I open my door just as a woman is getting out of a yellow Datsun next to us, and the sound of the two metal doors colliding is so loud that everyone close by looks over, including two boys about my age. They look puffy, and I notice they are wearing two coats apiece and they're all rumpled like they've been sleeping in the back of that station wagon for weeks.

The woman in the Datsun is checking the damage to her door, and Sister Josephine has come around to look at mine. "Good thing we all have rusty old cars," the nun says cheerfully, and the Datsun woman suddenly reminds me of a colorful paint-by-number with her flowered boots and lipstick, compared to Sister Josephine in her black tunic and her habit. If the woman had thought of blaming me for denting her door, she obviously isn't going to anymore. Who argues with a six-foot nun? She shrugs and steers the boys inside the store, but the older one looks back at me with a quizzical expression on his face.

"Well," says Sister Josephine, "you wanted to come to town so badly; are you going to hide in the truck now?"

Her eyes are twinkling.

"Will you tell me more about my gran before we get back to the convent?"

"Help me get these soaps and lotions inside, and we'll see," she says.

The mercantile is one of those out-of-the-way places that has a bit of everything. Pump pots full of coffee and hot-pink Hostess Sno Balls are the "breakfast special." There's a whole wall of fishing lures and metal spinner racks of postcards with pictures of moose or pristine mountain lakes. The dusty cans of peas and fruit cocktail could be ten years old, it's hard to say. There is another aisle with playing cards, panty hose, and votive candles mixed in with just about everything else that nobody needs. This is also the aisle where the nuns sell their soaps and lotions. It seems pretty well stocked to me, but Sister Josephine says to squeeze in as many more as I can. The label says PERPETUAL SORROW SOAP, and I wonder if the nuns should think about changing the name.

"Here's my own special milk-and-honey lotion," she says, making a precarious pyramid with a few of the bottles.

I glance over at the Datsun woman, who has come out of the bathroom looking a bit tidier. Her hair is freshly combed and her lips are much, much redder than when she was frowning at me for denting her door. The boys have decided on the breakfast special, and the older one is stirring his coffee with a red plastic straw and stealing looks at me. I pull my jacket tight around my belly and pretend to be busy. But I can hear everything they say.

"How much farther to Fairbanks?" asks the younger boy,

his mouth full of Sno Ball. The word *Fairbanks* is like a kick in the gut, which the baby decides to do just then, right on cue. "Shhh," I tell it, rubbing my belly.

"It's a good week," says the woman, pouring coffee into a foam cup.

"Well, we've been driving for two weeks already," says the older boy. "That doesn't seem so bad."

"It wouldn't take so long if they'd pave the road," she says, "but the Alaskan side doesn't want to spend the money and the Canadian side doesn't want to spend the money. So nobody does it."

"Well, I can drive, too," the boy says, "if you want a break."

"Thanks, Oscar. We'll see."

He doesn't look like an Oscar to me. It sounds old-fashioned. He needs a haircut. I watch him push his bangs out of his eyes every few seconds. His hair is dirty and it's obvious he hasn't showered in a while; he moves slowly, like he's carrying the world on his shoulders. But there is something sweet about his disheveled appearance. If he washed his hair, it might be the same color as Ray's. I shake my head at the thought of Ray and how quick I am to think this stranger looks sweet.

Aren't all boys the same? I've only been at the convent for about a month, but it feels like years and I've forgotten what people my own age look and act like. Then again, maybe I've never known. I wouldn't be here now if I'd been smarter.

I watch Oscar watching his little brother, who has a

rounder face than him and darker hair and skin, but they have the same sharp, pointy nose and the same dirty, tousled look. The younger one is licking his Sno Ball–covered lips, which are pink and chocolaty with bits of coconut stuck to them. Oscar hands him a napkin, but he's also smiling in such a sweet brotherly way—there is nothing phony about it. It reminds me of when George gave me a doughnut that day at the Salvation Army and how strangers have been kinder to me than my own family. Suddenly I feel like the loneliest person in the world. Without any warning, I know I have to get out of here. I drop all my soaps in a heap and bolt out of the store, the little bell tinkling as if to alert the world that I have just been completely undone by the smallest act of kindness.

In the truck I can't stop crying. Sister Josephine comes out and hands me a travel packet of tissues and a lumpy brown package with my name on it. The boy called Oscar has come out to stare at us as we pull away. I slump farther down in my seat, but the tears will not stop.

Sister Josephine does not go back to Our Lady of Perpetual Sorrow right away. She pulls off onto a secluded dirt road and bumps along until we reach the river. She stops the engine and we sit watching the muddy water roll past. I'm sniffling and wondering how she knew this secret spot was here when, as if reading my mind, she says, "Your gran and I used to come here all the time."

She points through the trees and I can see the brick out-line of the convent. I wonder if she means they somehow got here by crossing the river from the other side. That would be pretty adventurous, and I wonder what else I don't know about who Gran once was.

Sister Josephine's wimple and habit make it seem as if she is looking through a curtained window, straight ahead so I can't see her face. I realize she's not staring at the river; she's looking into the past.

"I was nineteen. Your gran was probably sixteen. I was trying to decide if I had a calling, and she was trying des-perately to get out of here. Sister Agnes warned me that she was a bad influence, but Marguerite was so funny and char-ismatic, it was hard not to want to be around her."

I would never use any of those words to describe Gran.

"She'd lived her whole life here. Her mother died. Her fa-ther couldn't take care of her. Or maybe he just wouldn't. She was only three when he left her with the abbess. I don't think your gran ever got over that feeling of being aban-doned, even though the abbess took a shine to her like you wouldn't believe."

I think about Gran taking in me and Lily after Dad died. I never thought about how hard that must have been for some-one her age—a five-year-old and a brand-new baby.

Sister Josephine swivels her white neck to look at me, a huge smile on her face. "Oh, the abbess loved your gran like she was her own child—always called her their precious gift from God." She chuckles. "Sister Agnes, as I'm sure you've realized, has never understood their relationship. We're just human, but people think we aren't going to feel normal emotions once we get professed. Jealousy, anger, sorrow. When your gran left in the middle of the night without saying good-bye, even the abbess couldn't pretend that her heart wasn't a tiny bit broken."

Ironically, Gran reminds me more of Sister Agnes than the abbess.

"But she must have kept in touch; otherwise, how did I get here?" I ask.

"She did, oh she did. But it was mostly in times of need. I think that's part of what bothers Sister Agnes so much. When your mother got ill—after your father died—your gran asked Mother Superior if there was a place that would take her in so she didn't have to be put in a home. She wasn't right in the head after that."

Sister Josephine looks like maybe she's said too much; her face turns pink against the white of her wimple. "Oh, Ruth, I'm so sorry about your father."

"I'm starting to forget him," I tell her. "And my mother."

"It's like that sometimes, isn't it? Your family seems to have some kind of snowball effect going on," she says sadly.

"That's one way of saying it," I tell her, blowing my nose into one of the tissues. "Instead of a curse, I mean; a snowball effect sounds almost nice."

I think about the pink Sno Ball that boy was eating back at the mercantile and the way his brother was looking at him. What is their story? I know I should care more about my own family, but our story will always be old and tired and badly written. If I had the energy, I would try to rewrite it. Perhaps Lily will be the one to do that.

But even if I am following in the footsteps of my mother and my grandmother, there's still a part of me that believes I deserve better. I would give anything for someone to look at me the way Oscar looked at his brother, covered in a pink Hostess Sno Ball. I almost tell Sister Josephine right there on the bank of the river why I broke down back at the mercantile, but it seems silly. How do you find words to describe that much emptiness?

"Aren't you going to open your package? It's the first mail you've received," says Sister Josephine.

I look at the loopy handwriting and realize it's from Selma. Good old Selma, writing to me when I didn't even say goodbye to her. I slowly unwrap it and out falls a lumpy, hand-knitted hat. It's orange, of course, and extremely large.

Dear Ruth,

Your gran called the other day and gave me your address; she thought you might like news from home. Wasn't that nice? My knitting gauge is still a little off, but I made this for your baby anyway. I hope it gets there in time so he/she can take it with them to their new family. (I think orange can be good for a boy or a girl, right?) I know it won't fit until the baby is probably grown up, but I thought it would be nice to have something so they'd have a little connection to their first family. We don't have to be blood to be family. (I can see you rolling your eyes, don't think I can't!)

I think what you're doing is really brave. I know you're frustrated with me, and I know you feel that always thinking the best of people isn't that easy, but I'm just going to go ahead and keep disagreeing with you. It really is that easy. I still think the best of you and I think your baby will, too—when they're old enough to understand. I hope it doesn't hurt too much and that you get to come home soon.

Love,
Selma

CHAPTER TEN

That Damn Blue Note

DORA

Over the past couple of weeks, fish camp has been non-stop busyness. Relatives just keep showing up, bringing their boats with wide hulls and their elders with wide, calloused hands, who have been cleaning fish for almost a hundred years. The camp is now full to the brim with wild boy cousins who roll around in the dirt and aunties with empty spaces in their mouths that make it hard to chew the dried fish, so they just suck on it all day long. For some reason there is always enough of everything, even places to sleep.

Dumpling's mom makes the same joke every day—"got to keep working till the sun goes down"—and everyone laughs, out of respect.

But kids here aren't really expected to work all the time

and the adults never push or nag us—so nobody says we have to stay and help instead of going into the village. There are so many people at fish camp—there's always someone around to stoke the fire or help Dumpling's mom—so it's not like we'll be missed. Dumpling's father has to get some parts for the outboard again, so Dumpling, Bunny, and I come along.

"Auntie says you can borrow the three-wheelers, at least until the gas runs out," he tells us. Maybe he just wants us out of his hair, but that's fine with us.

Once we see the three-wheelers, we forget everything that is going on back at camp. We tear up and down the main street of the village with the dirty wind in our hair, no purpose whatsoever other than to make a lot of noise and go really fast.

When I try to keep up with Dumpling, all I can see is her red ribbon waving at me like a flag. The mud from her back tires spits me with gravel pellets if I get too close; I have to slow down, and then I spray Bunny on her three-wheeler behind me and she yells as if she's been shot with a BB gun. We drive back and forth on the main street until only the whites of our eyes pop out of our mud-splotched faces.

"Damn village kids!" a priest yells as we spray him, too.

"I want to go back to the skiff," Bunny tells Dumpling when we finally nose our three-wheelers close enough to talk to each other. Dumpling has turned off the main street and taken us a ways from town, close to the slough. The wind is stiffer over here with no buildings around for shelter. The bent beach grass looks just like the hunched-over aunties in their kuspuks, waiting for us back at fish camp.

Dumpling hops off her three-wheeler and walks slowly toward three white clapboard houses sitting off by themselves: one with blue trim; one with a big, muscular dog in front; and one with a curtain that seems to be moving by itself every couple of seconds, behind broken glass. She tramps along the edge of the slough and up the bank. I follow, hoping she's watching out for dogs. Village dogs are always charging out from behind outhouses or woodpiles when you least expect it. There was a funeral the night we got here. Three-year-old Willard Hunter wandered out into his family's dog yard and got his face bitten off before anybody noticed he'd even slipped outside. Dogs and drowning are the two things Dumpling and Bunny are supposed to watch out for. I tighten the straps on my life jacket. Bunny is wearing one, too, but I notice Dumpling left hers back in the skiff.

"What are you looking for?" Bunny asks, running up and grabbing her hand.

Dumpling doesn't seem to hear Bunny as she walks up to the house with blue trim. In the yard sits a statue of a woman holding a baby, wrapped in an old sheet or maybe a tablecloth. The statue is covered with bird poop. Dumpling looks like she is trying to decide whether to go up the steps, when the priest we splattered with mud comes walking up.

"I can't imagine you're really here to apologize," he says.

We all look down at our muddy boots and jeans. But he surprises us and laughs.

"No harm done. You don't think you're the first kids to do that to me, do you?"

I glance sideways at Dumpling, but she's still looking at her feet.

"Can I invite you in for tea?" he asks. "Or maybe a soda?"

Dumpling shrugs, and I'm surprised that he understands this means yes. Why was Dumpling looking for this place? What could she possibly want to talk to a priest about? Bunny keeps staring at the woman with the baby, so I grab her arm to steer her up the stairs while the priest holds open the screen door for us.

"I'm Father Connery," he says, taking off his boots and sliding into a pair of gray slippers. He tells us to leave our boots in the arctic entryway and follow him into the kitchen. Dumpling tries to hide the hole in her sock as we stand in the doorway.

"Tea or soda?" he asks, pulling things out of white cupboards: a plate, cookies, pilot bread, and cheese. Dumpling gives Bunny the hairy eyeball, meaning "behave," and it makes Bunny instantly grumpy.

Father Connery looks at us and smiles. "Scared of me?" Dumpling pushes Bunny closer to the table, where he's put all the snacks, and I nudge in behind them. We all try to squish into the same chair.

"There're plenty of seats," he says as he gestures around the table. I move into an empty one, but Bunny stays with Dumpling, one butt cheek hanging off the edge. He sits down and pours tea. All of us would much rather have soda, but nobody says anything. He must be used to village kids not talking, but he tries to strike up a conversation anyway.

"So were you girls looking for someone special?"

Bunny is plopping sugar cubes into her cup, one after another, until Dumpling reaches out and grabs her wrist. Bunny can be very unpredictable if she thinks Dumpling is bossing her around, and sure enough, she pipes up and says to Father Connery, "Why does that lady in the yard not want the baby she's holding?"

Dumpling and I exchange looks.

"What makes you think she doesn't want her baby?" he asks, amused.

You can tell he's trying hard not to smile. Dumpling keeps her hand on Bunny's wrist.

Bunny shrugs and says, "Her face, I guess. It's like when we get a spawned-out salmon in the fish wheel and nobody wants to touch it."

I'm pretty sure Bunny is being sacrilegious.

"Well, I don't think anyone's ever said that before," says Father Connery. "Maybe the sculpture just doesn't do her justice. Do you know who that woman is?"

"A white lady?" Bunny says, as if that's the best she can do. I roll my eyes. Would Bunny have said that if Lily had been here? Probably, I think.

But Father Connery seems to find Bunny charming. "Yes, she is a white lady. She lived a very long time ago."

"She's the mother of God," says Dumpling. It's not like Dumpling to talk around strangers. Bunny and I stare at her.

"Yes, in a way. That's the Holy Mary," says Father Connery.

"God is a *baby*?" Bunny is stunned.

"It's a long story," Dumpling mutters, and looks over at me as if I can somehow help steer the conversation somewhere else. We both heard Lily trying to explain this to Bunny, but obviously it didn't stick. Lily said that Jesus was the baby and his father was God. Because he was God he could put Jesus inside of Mary and she didn't have to do anything nasty (which is how Lily said it), and Bunny was sure that was the bit about the man's private parts. If Bunny brings that up now in front of this priest, I swear I will kill her.

"Can I have a soda?" I ask.

"Oh, of course!" Father Connery jumps up to get it.

Dumpling digs her fingernails into Bunny's wrist as a final warning. She gives me a look like maybe we should think about leaving, but just then the door opens and two elderly women step inside. They have crosses around their necks and long black robes. Their faces are red and they have little beads of sweat on their foreheads—possibly because they're wearing black hoods that look like towels on top of their heads.

They smile at us and say hello, as if they always come home to find kids eating their crackers and drinking their tea.

"You three must be from the fish camp upriver," the shorter one says.

Dumpling nods but doesn't look up. She's suddenly very interested in the blue pattern on the china cup.

"Well, I'm Sister Mary Pat and this is Sister Mary Louise. Welcome." The one talking is skinny and wrinkled, but her eyes are sparkly and kind, like ripe berries. The other woman, who just nods and reaches for a cookie, is plumper and less wrinkled, and her glasses are so thick it's hard to see her eyes at all. I wonder if all nuns are called Sister Mary something-or-other.

"We should really get going," Dumpling says. "They're probably waiting for us in the skiff." She pulls Bunny up by the shoulder just as Bunny grabs my soda and spills it everywhere. We all look with horror at the mess, but nobody else seems concerned.

"Easy there, what's your rush?" says Father Connery. "Was there something you wanted to ask?"

But Dumpling is now hell-bent on getting us out of there. She's fumbling with her boots and Bunny and I are trying to get into ours as well—made even more complicated by Bunny's juggling of the soda can, which by now has left a sticky trail all the way to the door.

"Thanks for the tea," Dumpling mumbles.

And then we're outside, Dumpling's grip tight on Bunny's arm, steering us past the statue and down to the slough where we left the three-wheelers.

I look back and see Father Connery and the two nuns standing outside, watching us. I lift my hand to wave just as another person comes out of the house. A woman in jeans with a black ponytail. Where did she come from?

Dumpling starts up her three-wheeler and turns to make sure Bunny is getting onto hers, when she notices the woman on the steps. They stare at each other and then Dumpling turns the key and the engine sputters and dies again. She slides off the three-wheeler without even looking at me and walks back up to the house. The woman seems to sense something, moving like a wild deer, hesitant but forward, as if she's sniffing Dumpling out. I slide off my three-wheeler as well and follow, baffled.

"My dad said I might find you here," Dumpling says when the two are standing face to face. "I have a note from Ruth."

This surprises both me and the woman, who looks at Dumpling like she isn't sure she can believe her. "She asked me to give you this."

Dumpling holds out a piece of blue paper that she's pulled from her pocket—the same one I saw Ruth give her the night she left on the bus. The woman looks at it for a long time, but her eyes are unfocused.

"What is it?" says the woman. Her voice sounds like cottonwood fluff blowing in the wind.

"It's from Ruth."

"Ruth?" the woman says. "Ruth is only five years old."

My mind is trying to catch up with what is happening. Dumpling could have at least told me. I notice Bunny is just as surprised as I am.

"Have you seen her do ballet?" the woman is saying. "When her daddy gets home, Ruth is going to dance for him. We're just waiting for his plane to land."

"I can take that, dear," says one of the Marys. She has swooped down with her winglike robes not making a sound.

She reaches out to take the blue paper, but Dumpling won't let it go.

"I promised only to give it to Ruth's mother."

Ruth's mother?

"It's okay, dear. We can sort this out." The sister has her arms around the woman with the blank eyes, who is trying desperately to focus. The effort looks painful.

"Please," Dumpling whispers. "I promised."

And then a tear streaks down my friend's dry, dusty cheek. It reminds me of the river that we should be skiffing up right now, going to fish camp, where everything makes sense and smells of laughter and smoke, and where Dumpling will stop being sad about some promise she made to Ruth, who she is barely friends with anyway. The shock of seeing that tear has turned to anger.

"Come on, Bunny, let's get back to the skiff," I say as I grab her arm.

But now Bunny is staring at the woman, too. "If you're Ruth's mother, then you must be Lily's mother, too," she says. "Do you remember Lily?"

The woman stares at Bunny as if she's staring at a ghost. "Lily?"

And then without warning she lets out a loud piercing howl, as if she just stuck her finger in an electric socket, and lunges at Dumpling. I grab Bunny's arm and pull her away as both nuns now throw their arms around the woman, trying to calm her. Dumpling shoves the note into my hand and says, "Go; take Bunny to the skiff."

As she says it her head is jerked backward, because the woman has grabbed her braid, and Father Connery comes running down the steps to help.

Just when I think it can't get any worse, Bunny starts kicking the woman in the shins, yelling at her to let go of her sister.

"Get Bunny out of here!" Dumpling yells at me. I drag a flailing Bunny to the three-wheeler and have a hell of a time trying to hold on to her while starting it up. I have to leave Bunny's three-wheeler behind, because I can't trust her to follow me on her own.

When I turn to look, I can see Father Connery and the nuns pulling the woman up the stairs of the little white house. Dumpling is running toward her three-wheeler, so I know she's safe. Part of me hopes she got scratched herself. Since when did she make promises to Ruth?

"Here she comes, Bunny," I say, and she stops screaming and flopping around like a fish on a hook. "You didn't help," I add, but there's no point lecturing at her now; the three-wheeler is too loud. Making sure to hold Bunny's arms tight around my waist, we fly full throttle back to where the skiff is docked and Dumpling's father is waiting for us.

"Dumpling's right behind us," I tell him breathlessly as he lifts Bunny onto the skiff and she starts wailing again. I let her try to explain what just happened, and it's even more unintelligible than the truth.

"She didn't even remember Lily," Bunny says, as if this

mattered most. Her face is streaked with mud and tears and there is a fresh scratch on her arm.

Her father looks thoroughly confused, so I say, "Dumpling will just have to tell you when she gets here."

But Dumpling never shows up.

Now Bunny and I are sitting behind her father as he drives the three-wheeler back over the fresh, weaving tracks we made just minutes before. Something is pressing hard into my chest, and every minute that Dumpling does not appear makes it harder and harder for me to breathe. In the distance we see it—the upside-down three-wheeler looking so strangely out of place. My mind refuses to believe it. Maybe it's just a rock, or perhaps a bear rolling around on its back? The front wheel is still spinning in the air. Something is terribly wrong. Bunny is strangely silent while her father spurs our three-wheeler forward, everyone's hearts beating so loud we can almost hear them over the roar of the engine.

Dumpling's braid pokes out from under the metal body of the three-wheeler. Her arms and legs are pinned, her eyes are closed, and she is not moving.

"Dumpling!" Bunny yells, but her father says, "Stay back, Bunny," and is off the three-wheeler before we're even fully stopped. I'm paralyzed by fear, watching him bend down over Dumpling, the handlebar of the three-wheeler blooming out of her chest like a strange plant. For the second time in less than half an hour, I am left alone with a wildly out-of-control Bunny. But this time I just let her wail because I am powerless to move.

Other three-wheelers appear out of nowhere. The village has its own version of telephones: silent messages waft through the air and hang over every house during a crisis, and every able-bodied person comes to help.

The engines compete with Bunny's cries, as more and more people arrive on the scene. They position themselves to lift the three-wheeler off Dumpling in one swift motion, moving together as if they have done this a hundred times. I hope that isn't true.

Even without the weight pinning her down, nobody dares to move Dumpling. Her father kneels beside her and whispers in her ear, reminding me of the way he sat with her on the merry-go-round and how it made me feel alone. Was it just minutes ago that I hoped she was all scratched up by Ruth's mother? I want to take that back, along with every other bad and selfish thought I've ever had, if she would just sit up.

Someone says something about a plane and a medevac, but mostly it's now deathly quiet. Even Bunny has stopped wailing. Kids are expected to never be in the way, but now it seems even more important that Bunny and I stand back unnoticed. We watch her father hold Dumpling's head and neck stable while everyone else runs around talking into radios and zooming back and forth from town, bringing blankets and water and first-aid kits.

Father Connery arrives, driving Bunny's three-wheeler,

which we left behind. For a minute I imagine Bunny flying at him the way she did at that woman, but she's too
busy watching the medical team, who are carefully loading
Dumpling onto a stretcher and into a plane.

It appeared like magic—landing on the narrow strip of
gravel, bouncing its rubber wheels like basketballs on the
ground, and filling the air with dust, making it impossible
to see anything. None of us has ever flown on a plane before,
and I hope Dumpling will wake up so she can tell us about
it later.

Adults usually ignore us kids, so it's no surprise that
nobody pays attention to me and Bunny now, but I wish I
could at least get close to Dumpling. If I could just talk to
her. Maybe if she heard my voice she'd wake up, but fear of
being in the way is stronger and I stay rooted, holding on to
Bunny's shoulder for support.

Father Connery is talking in a hushed voice with Dumpling's dad. The two seem to know each other. The priest talks,
his hands folded; Dumpling's dad nods a few times, and then
Father Connery hugs him and Dumpling's dad gets into the
plane, too. It taxis down the road like a fat goose, then rises
precariously into the air, leaving me and Bunny alone.

She pulls herself together first. "We need to tell Mama,"
she whispers.

Her mom is back at fish camp, probably watching the
wobbly plane, not knowing that her daughter and husband
are on it. I picture her looking up at the sound of the engine, shielding her eyes from the sun with the ulu she's

been sharpening, getting ready to fillet another washtub of salmon and hang them in strips to dry.

We'll need to pack up the whole fish camp early so we can get home to Dumpling. Now there won't be enough salmon to last all year, but if Dumpling doesn't wake up, salmon will be the last thing on our minds this winter anyway.

CHAPTER ELEVEN

If You Must Smoke, Smoke Salmon

ALYCE

The king salmon opening is almost over, and Dad says he's heard a rumor about Sam's brothers. They got off the ferry, but he's not sure how or where. He's on the radio all the time now, trying to figure it out without giving Sam away. It's a tricky dance, and I can tell Sam is nervous. Every time the radio static cackles through the speakers, he jumps.

I've lost all track of real time, which is what happens on a boat. You forget everything and everyone that isn't right here, bobbing around in this small space of forty-six feet. For the most part, I mean. I still sometimes rehearse telling Dad that I've got to fly back to Fairbanks soon, because of the dance audition, but only in my head.

The sense of urgency on the boat is electric right now, Dad

and Uncle Gorky focused on helping Sam; Sam wondering and worrying about his brothers. I know I should care, too, that he finds them, and I do, but if Dad and Uncle Gorky can get this invested in helping him, why can't they see that I might have other things in my life, too, besides this boat?

At the moment Sam is wearing an old gray sweatshirt of Dad's and an even older pair of green rain pants that are rolled up three times so he doesn't trip over them. He has fish blood all over his face from getting too close to the bloodline when he scrapes it. It's a beginner problem, but I don't say this. Over the past week, I've noticed that I don't really look at Sam anymore so much as drink him up. I am trying not to be obvious.

He smiles and my stomach goes wobbly. We must have hit the wake of another boat, I tell myself, trying not to stare at the brown mole on Sam's lip, which at this moment is blending into the other reddish-brown spots of fish blood splattered across his face.

"Okay, well, I'm done with my ten fish over here. Maybe we should run the gear again," I say.

We have already fallen into that teasing banter that happens fast on boats. Sam has learned most of the jobs quickly, but I still clean twice as many fish as he does. I've never been the most experienced one on the boat before, and it's like watching my old self back when I only got to do the humpies: disgusting, stinky pink salmon that are small and not worth a lot of money. They also poop out gray slime every-where, which I used to think was cool, but not anymore.

Sam reminds me of what it was like to be curious about fishing, rather than bored. But then I see my dad looking at us quizzically from the wheelhouse doorway. I'm not sure if he's thinking about the fish or the fact that his daughter is standing in the troll pit laughing with a boy she pulled from the ocean. I prefer to believe he's thinking about the fish.

"I'll finish that one up, Sam. Here, give me your knife." If the fish aren't cleaned quickly, they turn stiff as a board, and then we get a lower price. But something tells me the look on my dad's face right now has very little to do with salmon.

Sam returns to running the gear, flipping the hydraulics that pull in the fishing lines like he's been doing it for years. He runs all four lines that are trolling behind the boat, grab-bing each hook as it goes by and clipping it onto the rail on the stern in a straight little line. Hoochies flap on the ends of the hooks—rubber squid made of all different colors and sizes—to entice the fish. "When I was a kid I used to name them," I say, "but I got lazy and after a while they were all just called Spot." He smiles at me. Since when did crooked teeth ever make me feel like this?

When Sam sets the gear again, he holds up each hoochie and says, "Name?" I throw out whatever comes to mind—Petey, Pinky, Fatty, Dogface—but he likes naming them after poets. "Whoever heard of a hoochie named Emily Dick-inson?" I ask him, and he just says, "Whoever heard of nam-ing a hoochie at all?"

Sam's strong enough to land kings, so Dad lets us do all the work if we aren't too slammed. Uncle Gorky still does all the icing in the fish hold, and he helps us clean if we get into a thick patch. I know Dad would rather sit in the wheelhouse eating peanuts and talking to *Sunshine* Sam on the radio. Every so often he dumps the shells out the window and they float past us, bobbing along on the waves as a reminder, to me, anyway, that there are more people than just me and Sam on this boat.

"So . . . what about those ballet slippers?" Sam asks, slapping a bright-red coho onto the deck; its scales glint silver and black in the sun, reflecting off the aluminum bait shed like disco lights.

The fish flaps around, hitting the bin boards a few times, until I stab it in the gills with a knife and blood pools out onto the black mat.

I don't say anything. I'm out of practice talking about myself on this boat.

I grab the fish's tail and slide it to the side so it can bleed all the way out.

"It's really pretty, isn't it?" Sam says, pointing his orange glove at the bloody mat. Streaks of red are smeared against the black rubber background, and they remind me of a tuxedo cummerbund or a fiery red sunset. I was going to rinse it off to keep the blood from splashing us when we land more fish, but the look on his face makes me pause. "What do you see?" he asks me.

"Blood?" I say. The words *tuxedo* and *sunset* suddenly seem too ridiculous, as if I'm talking about a prom date rather than a dead fish.

"It looks like the tail feathers of a huge tropical bird," he says, a true poet.

I spray the hose and the blood pools into the far corner, flowing out through the vents and into the ocean. Sam looks into my eyes and says, "You must miss dancing if you've hung your slippers up above your bunk."

I shift in my rubber boots. After standing for hours on a cement deck with cold water rushing over them, my feet are chunks of ice.

"I bet you're really good . . . ," he says cautiously, sensing that it's a sensitive topic. "A good dancer, I mean."

"I could be," I admit, yanking my eyes away from his. "The auditions are happening in early August, and if I want to get into a college dance program, I have to be accepted this summer. It's a small window to make it as a dancer. But it's right in the middle of fishing season, so it's not going to happen. But," I add hastily, "it's not that big a deal."

This could be the biggest lie I've ever told, and he's not buying it.

"Does your dad even know about it?"

I'm afraid I'll start crying. It really does seem like a stupid thing to cry over. Doesn't anybody understand that I feel like even *asking* is letting my dad down? Why does that seem so obvious to me, and so dumb to people like Sally and Izzy and Selma—and now Sam? But he doesn't actually say that. He doesn't say anything.

Instead he pulls me in close, and I think for a minute that he's going to kiss me.

"You've got some blood on your nose," he says, wiping my face with an orange-gloved finger. "Oops, I think I just made it worse."

"Well," I say, "you're pretty bloody yourself. Here, let me help you."

And without warning I lift the hose and spray him right in the face. He shouts and grabs the other hose, and a full-on water fight ensues. Out of the corner of my eye, I see Dad shake his head and shut the wheelhouse door to keep the damage contained on the back deck. Just as he ducks inside, though, I watch a shadow cross his face. How much of that did he just hear?

Later we anchor up in Crawfish Inlet and Dad says we can take the *Pelican* out and paddle around before dinner. It's supposed to blow tonight, so we pulled the gear early and got inside to shelter, but so far there isn't a hint of what the forecast promised. Sam asks if he can row, so I lie back and trail my hand over the side, watching the water ripple past.

"This is my favorite place," I tell him. "I shot my first deer up on that ridge. From the top you can see all the islands within spitting distance. When I die, I want my ashes scattered here."

"You're the weirdest ballerina I've ever met."

I watch him as he rows the raft that saved him. He is

wearing my uncle's sweatshirt that says IF YOU MUST SMOKE, SMOKE SALMON. It's weird to see this boy in my family's clothes—as if we've created him out of nothing. Or we're making him into something because he is our found object. *My* found object. I push away the thought that it's probably very unfair to do that to someone.

"You okay?" I ask him.

He shrugs—another gesture he picked up from my dad and uncle. Maybe it comes with the clothes.

"You can tell me," I say, but I sound pushy.

He looks at me and his lips form a half-smile. I never knew how much I liked being noticed before, being smiled at. Even partially smiled at.

"Old habit . . . ," he says, and then stops.

I wait. He is struggling to find words, which I already know is unusual for him.

"Ever since my dad went missing, I felt like I was being disloyal if I didn't think about him every single minute . . ." The pauses between his sentences are so long, I hold my breath waiting for him to finish. "But I get it, he's really gone."

"I'm sorry about your dad" is all I can think to say.

"It's not that. It's just . . . I figured Hank was mad at me, but it seems like a long time for him not to try to find me. Maybe he didn't see me get rescued. What if he thinks I'm dead?"

"Oh."

I should say something, but what? What did I expect he was thinking? That he's never had so much fun in his life, cleaning fish and smelling humpy poop and being with me? What did I think he was, a stray puppy? *Daddy, can I keep him?*

"Well, my dad could call the ferry again." I try not to sound like I hoped he was thinking about me.

"Are you jealous?" he says. But it sounds like a statement, not a question.

"Of course I'm not."

"Really? You seem like it. A tiny bit?"

I flick water at him from the side of the boat, trying to hide what he clearly sees.

"Watch it," he says. "These are probably the last dry clothes anyone is going to lend me."

This is definitely true, so I stop.

"Tell me about your brothers," I say.

Why do I keep lying? I get it that he's going to think about his brothers, but every time it feels like we might be getting closer, he pulls away. Is it wrong that I want him to say he's thrilled that I saved him and he's never been happier, and then I want him to shut up and kiss me already?

"I think you should tell your dad that you want to dance," he says. "It's obvious how much he loves you—he'd just want you to be happy."

I don't know if I'm angry at him all of a sudden because I'm embarrassed about my obvious feelings, or sad that he's going to leave soon. Or maybe I wish my dad would help me get what I want, as much as he's trying to help Sam.

"You've been on this boat for less than two weeks, and you think you know us?" I snap.

He looks stunned. I'm surprised, too, at how my words crack out of my mouth like a whip. I don't sound like myself at all.

But I've kept my nose out of his business; I haven't asked what he was running away from or why he was even on the side of that ferry anyway. Now he's trying to tell me what to do, like he knows *my* dad better than I do?

"You're talking to me like I'm an idiot," he says.

"Idiot is a bit strong; maybe you're just overly optimistic about how easy it is to talk to my dad." I try to calm down, to not sound mean.

How did this go so terribly wrong?

"Well, you should meet my brother Jack someday," he says, turning the *Pelican* to port and heading back to where the *Squid* is anchored. "He makes me look like a pessimist."

I've hit a nerve with him, too.

"My life's just kind of . . . complicated," I mumble.

"Yeah, I wouldn't know anything about that," he says. "Mine has always been cake."

He digs in hard with the oars as the clouds roll in and choppy waves slap against the *Pelican*.

We're climbing back on board the *Squid* when I hear the marine operator through the speaker on the deck. "Marine vessel *Matanuska*, calling fishing vessel *Squid*, do you copy?"

My dad answers, "This is W-A-J-eighty-four-eighty-five the *Squid*, channel ten?"

"Roger, channel ten."

He switches it away from sixteen, the Coast Guard emergency call channel, and over to ten. I imagine half the fleet is switching to ten as well. It's the fishermen's version of daytime soap operas, eavesdropping on everyone's marine radio calls.

Sam's face has gone an ashy-gray color, our little squabble forgotten.

I tie the *Pelican*'s bowline to the *Squid*'s stern, and we go stand outside the wheelhouse door. I don't think Dad heard us come back.

"So, those boys you wondered about? They turned themselves in," says a scratchy voice from deep inside the radio. "Prince Rupert."

"Are they headed back this way?" my dad asks.

"No, they had to be handed over to authorities and it's all private—looks maybe like some kind of domestic issue."

"How long ago?"

"About a week and a half."

Sam has been with us all that time, and I can see he's doing the math in his head, too.

"Any idea where they've been sent?"

"Looks like a social worker stepped in and they're moving them to Fairbanks. We were just going over the call logs and saw that you'd been asking."

Sam holds his breath.

I wait for my dad to say something about Sam, but he just shakes his head a little and says he thought he might know the boys, but he was wrong. "Thanks for the shout. W-A-J-eighty-four-eighty-five the *Squid*, clear."

Sam looks like he might need the bucket. But when my dad puts the mike back on the hook, Sam says adamantly, "Hank never would have turned himself in. Never."

The word *Fairbanks* echoes inside my head, like it's bouncing off the wheelhouse walls. They've been sent to my hometown?

Sam opens the wheelhouse door. "You didn't tell them about me," he says to my dad.

"It's not my secret to tell," Dad says, not at all surprised to see us. "I'd check with you first."

My dad is staring out the window. My mom left him because she said he wasn't capable of caring about people, just boats and engines and killing things. But she is wrong. I imagine rebuilding an engine is a hell of a lot easier than making decisions that affect other people's lives. And then it hits me: Dad's doing this for Sam because he knows I care about Sam. He's doing it for me.

"Do you want to go north and find your brothers?" he finally asks.

Sam just nods.

"We'll go to town tomorrow, then," Dad says. "You've worked hard enough to earn a plane ticket."

There's another interminably long pause as I think about Sam leaving. When Dad starts talking again, I can barely follow what he's saying.

"Alyce needs to get back to Fairbanks anyway, if she's going to make that audition. You two can fly north together."

"Dad?" But he's still looking out the window, not at me. I walk over and lean my head against his shoulder. His green

157

raincoat is wet and smooth and stinky, like an orca's nose. He smells of salt and wind and more love for me than I probably deserve. He pats my hair and, as if he's talking to the ocean, says, "You should have just asked."

"But how will you fish without me?" I whisper.

Uncle Gorky coughs loudly from the day bench. "I'm not totally useless," he says.

It's all too much for my dad, especially since I'm squeezing him so tight around the neck now that he can barely breathe.

CHAPTER TWELVE

Something to Look Forward To

HANK

I remember my dad saying that sometimes you can be inserted into another person's life just by witnessing something you were never really supposed to be a part of. I think about the chicken lady and how she may be the only person who saw what happened to Sam. It linked her to us in a weird way, even though she couldn't tell us anything.

Maybe that's happened with the pregnant girl that ran out of the mercantile, too—she was looking at me and then she just fell apart. Did I get inserted somehow into her story?

Isabelle is looking at the dent in the door of her beloved Datsun. "Being pregnant can make people very emotional," she says. "Not that I would know firsthand; that's just what they say."

She bends over and scratches some green paint off the yellow door with her key. "I don't think we can drive it like this." She tries to shut it, but it hangs crooked, refusing to latch. "Well, at least we're still in Canada. It's cheaper to fix it here. You don't mind, do you? One more day?"

I barely hear what Isabelle is saying. I'm too distracted thinking about that girl. I've never seen someone my age pregnant before. She *looked* young, anyway, running out the door with her blond ponytail bobbing behind her. On the ground right where the truck was is the red ribbon I noticed in her hair as she left.

I pick it up and stash it in my pocket. Isabelle keeps talking. "Maybe they have their babies young in this part of the world." She doesn't sound like a social worker. Aren't they supposed to care about things like teen mothers?

Jack raises an eyebrow, but grins just the same. Isabelle has grown on him, I can tell. He slips something square and heavy into my hand and then hops into the backseat of the car. PERPETUAL SORROW SOAP, the label says. It smells flowery.

"I'm going to look up a number for a mechanic," says Isabelle, heading over to the pay phone that's hanging askew on the outside wall of the mercantile. It doesn't look long for this world; she'd better hurry. I lean into the open window and whisper to Jack, "Are you saying I should wash with this for an uplifting experience?"

"That's what she and the nun were delivering in the store. They had boxes of those soaps. Read the back."

Our Lady of Perpetual Sorrow is an order of Roman Catho-

lic nuns whose main purpose is to live a simple life of worship and devotion to God through prayer, chastity, and solitude. We hope you enjoy our soaps.

"I didn't think nuns could get pregnant," Jack says, and I bonk him on the head with the soap.

"She isn't a nun, Jack."

"Oh, she's a soap maker, then?" He leans out of reach in case I don't like that idea, either.

I don't want to talk about this anymore. But if Isabelle wants to stay another day, maybe I can at least take her ribbon to her and see if she's okay.

"Our Lady of Perpetual Sorrow is the abbey on the road that heads west out of town," the man behind the counter says when I go back in the mercantile to ask. "But if you want their stuff, you have to buy it here. They're cloistered. No visitors."

"Oh, okay. I was just curious," I say nonchalantly.

The man surveys me under bushy eyebrows. "Of course, there's a little campsite on the river with a view of the abbey that only the locals know about. You aren't plannin' any vandalism or trouble for the nuns, are ya?"

"No, no, absolutely not. I was just interested in seeing what an abbey looks like."

"Well, you can see it through the trees on this side, and I have to say, you can hear the bells and listen to 'em singin' and it's quite lovely." He draws a little map on the back of a matchbook. "Don't make me regret givin' ya this."

"No, I promise. Thanks a lot."

We spend the night in the car right outside the auto body shop. Isabelle is a queen at sleeping while sitting straight up in the driver's seat. She's been sleeping like that all the way from Prince Rupert, over thirteen hundred miles. Jack and I put the backseat down and curl up together under a moth-eaten blanket, which Isabelle says could save our lives in a pinch.

A guy in greasy coveralls bangs on the window early the next morning, yelling as if he's had way too many cups of coffee, "Rise and shine. We're ready to fix your car."

I can tell Jack doesn't buy my excuse that I just want a quiet walk alone in the woods. I wouldn't, either. He gives me a look equivalent to being put through a lie detector test, which I'm sure I fail. But all he says is, "Lots of mosquitoes out there; have fun." He and Isabelle pull out the cribbage board that Phil gave him and prepare to spend the morning in a booth at the Gold Rush Diner.

It's a lot farther to the secluded road than it looks on the matchbook, and by the time I get there, I'm tired and sweaty and wondering what the hell I'm even doing. I'm also covered in bug bites. It's totally deserted, so I strip down and plunge my hot, sticky body into the river before more mosquitoes can get me, just as the abbey bells begin to chime.

The ribbon is balled up in my fist, and I swim out to the middle where I can just barely make out the outline of a brick building through the trees. The only problem is that the river gets shallower on the other side, so pretty soon

I'm walking in just knee-deep water over jagged rocks, hoping to God that this is truly as secluded as the man made it sound. On the opposite shore I'm immediately greeted by a cloud of mosquitoes thrilled to find so much naked skin.

I follow the sound of the abbey bells up an incline, careful to stay hidden in the scrubby spruce trees. This has got to be the most asinine thing I've ever done. I told the man back at the store that I had no intention of causing trouble; I hope walking naked around the abbey doesn't count.

Just a few yards away from where I'm hidden in the trees is a clothesline with some sheets and towels whipping in the breeze. I've lost my nerve and think I'll just tie the ribbon onto the clothesline and get out of here, when the pregnant girl comes walking toward it with a white basket pressed over her stomach.

She pulls off the wooden clothespins and tries to grab the corners of a white sheet, which is flapping on the line like a giant goose. I almost don't believe it myself when I hear my own voice say, "Uh, hey, hello there."

She spins around and gets totally tangled in the sheet.

"Who's there?" she yells, and then, almost as an afterthought, she says, "I have a knife. Don't you come near me."

I'm pretty certain she doesn't have a knife.

"I won't come near you," I say.

"Come out of the woods. Now!" she shouts.

"I don't think you really want me to do that."

"I'm going to call Mother Superior." She is backing slowly toward the abbey.

"No, please. I'll come out if you throw me the sheet."

"Are you some kind of pervert?" She's still trying to untangle herself.

I am definitely getting off on the wrong foot here.

"No, I was just swimming in the river and I—uh—well, my clothes are on the other side."

"You know what—forget Mother Superior, I'm going to get Sister Agnes and you're really going to be sorry."

"Okay, don't call anyone. I'll come out." I don't know who this Sister Agnes is, but if she's scarier than a Mother Superior, it can't be good. "And I really hope you were joking about that knife."

This is definitely the most embarrassing moment of my life, I think as I manage to grab a bouquet of wild bluebells and hold them in front of myself, edging slowly out of the trees.

"Can you throw me the sheet?" I plead.

She stares at me in disbelief. The good news is that people are far less likely to call for help if you look ridiculous. That's what I'm banking on, and thank God, she giggles.

"Oscar?" she says, her eyes sparking with recognition. She is beautiful when she smiles, I can't help noticing, despite the situation.

"Actually, that's not really my name," I say. "If you give me the sheet, I'll tell you what it is."

She thinks about this but takes one more long look at me, bluebells and all, as if committing the image to memory. Then she finally tosses me the sheet.

"You still can't come up here," she says as I wrap it around myself and she glances over her shoulder at the abbey. "Sister Agnes will have my head on a platter if there's a boy here. Especially one, well, obviously . . ." She trails off. "You have to get out of here."

I think about giving her the bluebells, but I'm afraid this might not be the right time, so I toss them aside.

"You dropped your ribbon," I say, holding out my hand so she can see it. What idiot would forge a river buck naked just to return a dirty ribbon? I can name only one.

"And I was wondering if you were okay," I add, lamely.

She looks back at the abbey, then gestures toward the trees.

"So, your real name?" she asks, once we get in a few yards.

"It's Hank," I tell her. "My brother is Jack." It seems important that she know our names. Even though I doubt I'll ever see this girl again.

I hold her hand to help her down the steep incline, trying not to trip on the sheet. The tiny beat of her pulse against my fingers surprises me. I wonder who touched her last, then feel like a jerk for thinking it.

"Want to sit?" I ask.

I can tell she's hesitant, but then she relents, "Okay, but just for a few minutes."

We plop down in the middle of a low-bush cranberry patch without saying anything. The red berries are staining the white sheet, and I wonder if she'll get in trouble for that, too. She picks some berries but doesn't talk at all. I'm sure the few minutes are already up.

"I'm just dealing with a lot," she says finally, glancing at her belly. "I'm sorry you had to see me . . . you know, lose it like that."

"It's fine."

But she doesn't say any more about what caused her to "lose it."

"Um—it's just that—you were looking over at us and then you sort of . . . you know . . . fell apart." I must sound nosy, or maybe vain, like I wanted it to be about me. But she doesn't answer anyway. Instead she changes the subject. "I'm from Fairbanks, the place you're headed. I heard your brother mention that yesterday."

She says it the way someone would say, "Lovely weather we're having."

"Is it nice there?" I ask.

God, I am making awkward small talk.

She shrugs.

I don't ask her why she is here, or if she is married, or what she is planning to do with her baby. For a second I wish I were Jack, who always sees the gossamer threads floating invisibly between people. They are so translucent, it's no wonder most people don't see them—or they bumble along and end up destroying them without ever knowing they existed.

"It was your brother," she says, cutting into my thoughts.

"Excuse me?"

"I mean . . . it was the way you were looking at him."

"How was I looking at him?"

"Like he meant something." Now she's the one who seems embarrassed. "I mean, to you. It just hit me—funny, you know?"

No, I don't know. But I don't say that. I've been so caught up in Sam going missing and making decisions for Jack and trying to be "the man of the family" that it surprises me how nice it is to talk to someone else about their life. Even though I really don't understand why me looking at Jack made her cry.

"Maybe I just miss being around people my own age," she mumbles.

I could ask her why she's here and a million other things, but instead I say, "Maybe I can see you in Fairbanks someday?"

She smiles.

"You mean, like something to look forward to?"

I nod. Why not?

"Ouch," she says, her hand suddenly flying to her stomach. "Sorry, I've got a little boxer inside me these days."

Her dress is stretched across her belly, and underneath it's *moving*, rippling like a taut canvas or a drum being played from the inside.

"That is so freaky," I say without thinking. But she doesn't seem to mind.

She smiles at me, and I hope she's never smiled at anyone like that before.

"I'm Ruth," she says, "Ruth Lawrence, and I should get back." I help her up. "I need the sheet, too." She smirks.

"But first, here." She ties the ribbon I've been holding around my wrist.

"Take this—because sometimes you just have to hold

167

on to whatever you can," she adds, mysteriously. Then she turns her back and waits.

I drop the sheet at her feet and whisper in her ear, "See you in Fairbanks, Ruth." I never take my eyes off her and she doesn't turn around, even when I am back in the middle of the river and I'm sure she can hear me splashing. She picks up the sheet, and I watch her slowly make her way back up the hill toward the abbey.

I'll never understand how certain things that happen to us can climb under our skin and make us someone new. Big things can do it—like Sam going missing. Small things can do it, too, like having a stranger fall to pieces right in front of you. I'm beginning to think that everything changes us to some extent.

I can't explain any of this to Jack, who is smart enough not to ask. But I catch him trying to size up the new bits of me that he can see around the edges of the person he's always known.

We sit very silent in the back of the yellow Datsun as it crawls slowly along the Alcan Highway, the muddiest, dirtiest, potholiest road you've ever seen. It's slow going. I just keep thinking about Ruth walking back up that hill alone. All the questions I didn't ask start to plague me, as she becomes less of a reality and more like something I dreamed up.

It takes almost two weeks to drive instead of the one Isabelle had expected, because of how bad the road is. We have four flat tires in the span of a week; we lose a whole day just sitting on the side of the road. We run out of gas and have to wait for someone to come by and give us a lift to the next station—and then a lift back. And we spend countless hours waiting in the middle of the road for things like mountain goats to cross so we can pass. Isabelle is thoroughly grumpy by the time we hit the outskirts of Fairbanks, partly from sleeping in the car with two smelly boys and partly because she's just realized she's going to have to drive it all again in reverse. Jack thinks she's sad that we won't be with her, but I think that's just Jack again.

Isabelle has grown on us, though, and when we see the sign that says WELCOME TO THE GOLDEN HEART CITY, a shadow falls inside the car. We pull into the parking lot of a dirty brick building.

"I have to go talk to this woman at the newspaper—alone," she says. "Can you guys just wait in the car?"

We stare out the window without talking, both of us wondering if Isabelle is inside sealing our fate, handing us off to another family.

There is a murky gray river and a white church with a pointy steeple perched on its bank. People meander by, waving casual greetings or pushing strollers; kids on bikes wobble between wary pedestrians, making them jump off the sidewalk. It's a busy town, full of construction workers and big, muddy trucks. And it's noisy.

"Is that girl keeping her baby?" Jack asks suddenly, watching a woman fiddle with the strings of her child's sun hat while the infant squirms and screams.

"Her name is Ruth Lawrence," I say, just so I can hear it

169

out loud, exactly the way she said it. "And I don't know, I didn't ask her."

I should have asked.

We keep watching the woman on the sidewalk as the infant pulls its hat off for the third time. The woman looks exasperated; both of them are red-faced and irritable.

Just watching this mother try to put on a hat looks like a nightmare. Being pregnant is one thing; a real, live, kicking human being is something else. I think of Ruth saying, *"I'm just dealing with a lot,"* and wonder if she thinks I was an ass not to ask her more about it.

Jack has pulled out the brown paper towel that Phil gave him and is tracing the thick black letters with his finger. He'd been doing it all across Canada. At one point I told him he was going to wear it out before we even got to Fairbanks.

"But it feels like the wing of a bird, or maybe a butterfly—it's addicting." He held it out to me to trace, but all I felt was a scratchy paper towel.

"You don't feel that?"

I gave him the look.

"I can't help it, Hank," he said, and he sounded so old for a fourteen-year-old boy.

I did not envy Jack.

"You could lie," he says, still tracing Selma's name.

"What do you mean?"

"Just lie and say you're eighteen so we don't have to live with a foster family."

"I can't, Jack. We can't risk them separating us and I don't want to get caught lying. I promised Phil we'd keep it honest after how much he helped us."

I stare at the sky. Canada geese are flying in a V shape overhead. It's August, but fall is right around the corner. Isabelle said it can come and go in just a day. I imagine the geese flying over the route we just drove, looking for warmer waters. Life would be so much easier with wings.

Right then Isabelle comes flying out of the newspaper building as if she's also a Canada goose, in a huge hurry to get somewhere. "My friend is at a ballet audition that's just starting. We need to meet her there."

"Isabelle, what about us?" I ask.

"What? You have an expiration date all of a sudden? You'll keep until after the ballet," she says.

Jack raises an eyebrow at me and shakes his head, but I know what he's thinking because I'm thinking it, too. We're both really going to miss her.

FALL

Fall is breaking into blossom;
The gold of devil's club and birch
The maroon of cranberries
The salmon and peach and flame of
Currant
And fire weed.

—ANN CHANDONNET

CHAPTER THIRTEEN

Bluebells in Whiskey Bottles

RUTH

It's been weeks since Selma's last letter telling me that Dumpling's in a coma. Worrying about Dumpling takes up all the extra space in my head, even the space I was using to wonder if Hank was really real. I want to call home and see how she is, but Sister Bernadette says international calls are strictly forbidden. I tried to write, but what would I say? And if Dumpling is in a coma, she wouldn't be able to read it anyway.

Dumpling, the only person who even bothered to say good-bye to me. Of course, Gran couldn't have come outside to wait for the bus the night I left Fairbanks, because what would the neighbors have thought? She had to teach me a lesson, and in some ways you had to admire how hard Gran sticks to her guns. It doesn't hurt any less, but it does help to understand where she's coming from.

I hadn't expected anyone to sit with me, but Dumpling had showed up on the merry-go-round, just like she'd done on the steps of the church as we watched the river.

Dumpling had this way of being there without saying anything that was so soothing. But that night I could hear the minutes ticking by in my brain, closer and closer to the time I'd have to get on that bus.

"I've seen my gran give your dad letters," I told her. I would normally have been embarrassed talking about my family like this, but I was desperate and I could hear the bus just a few streets away. The grinding gears and loud air brakes made my spine prickle; it was like hearing the future before you're ready to be in it.

Dumpling did not flinch. She also didn't pretend that her dad wasn't involved with my family in some way. Did she know about my parents? Did her dad talk to her in ways that Gran never talked to me? Or did she piece it together the same way I did—by watching her dad stop by every other week under the guise of being neighborly, bringing a fillet of salmon one day, some venison jerky another.

Gran would smile at him and exclaim over his generosity. Then she'd slide him a crisp white envelope with cramped handwriting, the address too small to read from a distance. He would tuck it into his Carhartt vest pocket and tip his hat to Gran respectfully. After a while I guessed it might be for Mama, because who else did Gran know? The look on Dumpling's face told me I'd probably guessed right.

"Do you think your dad might be okay with delivering a note from me, too?" I asked.

"I can ask him," she'd said with a shrug. But I could tell by the way she looked at me that she knew it was no small favor.

"Ruth, your mom isn't well. I don't think she would have left you and Lily if she could have helped it."

"Did your dad say that?"

She just nodded, but her eyes wouldn't meet mine. Nobody admits to talking about other people behind their backs; it's just not done.

When the bus arrived, I gave her the blue note and climbed on board. "Bye, Ruth." Her voice was so soft. It floated up the steps behind me like a tiny bird.

At a truck stop somewhere near the Canadian border, I turned seventeen all by myself. I used my emergency money that Gran gave me knotted up in the corner of a handkerchief to buy a Hostess apple pie as a birthday cake. The baby seemed to like it, or at any rate it woke up and played me like a bongo from the inside for the next few hours. I guess I wasn't truly alone on my birthday after all.

Now my thoughts about Dumpling squish right up against my anxiety about the impending birth. I'm tired of thinking only of myself, but I'm tired of worrying about Dumpling, too.

To keep myself busy, I ask if I can help out more in the kitchen. Sister Agnes still scares the pants off me, but I've learned that her bark is worse than her bite. Today she tells me that the abbess is having a private meeting and we should make scones and use the nice cups for tea.

I head out to pick blackberries for the scones—the bushes are loaded down and I pick my way through the woods overlooking the river. I sometimes feel like I imagined Hank being here in these woods, except that when I braid my hair the red ribbon isn't tied to the bottom of it anymore.

I'm deep inside my own head when a lime-green Gremlin drives up and parks in front of the abbey, alerting me to the fact that I've been daydreaming again. These must be the abbess's guests, and Sister Agnes is probably champing at the bit for the blackberries.

As I come through the woods, a man and a woman are getting out of the car. He is tall and wearing a plaid shirt like a lumberjack. She has fiery red hair and is wearing a springy dress with a peach cardigan that clashes a tiny bit with her hair. They look nice. She's carrying a bouquet of bluebells in a glass bottle. I think of Hank again, and I can't help but smile to myself. More proof that he was really here. (I couldn't have made up that part if I tried.)

There has been a stream of visitors like these over the past few weeks, although it seems that Sister Agnes finds a lot of things for me to do every time guests arrive. Keeping me and my belly hidden is proving more and more difficult every day.

I slip through the back door of the kitchen, where Sister Agnes is waiting. "What did you have to do? Grow them yourself?" she barks.

Sister Bernadette is preparing a tray with a white hand towel and three bone-china cups and saucers dotted with crimson flowers; she winks at me behind Sister Agnes's back.

"Shall I carry the tray in?" I ask, wiping the smile right off her face.

"Oh no, dear. I can do it," she says.

"I need you to go hang these towels on the line anyway," says Sister Agnes.

"But yesterday you said we were going to start hanging things inside, in the drying room."

"Well, that was yesterday," she snaps. I look out at the threatening clouds and decide to keep my mouth shut. She piles the hand towels in a basket and Sister Bernadette heads down the hall leading to Mother Superior's study.

I've only been in there once—the day I arrived. The room is very dark and smells like leather and wood oil and old books. The abbess is very old, too, but also very kind; her round face is papery and her skin is practically translucent, as if she's never seen the sun. She wears a heavy cross around her neck, which must be the reason she's slightly hunched over. I think she's been wearing it for almost a hundred years. She welcomed me and said she hoped I would be happy here, and that was the last time we spoke.

"Get a move on," Sister Agnes says, nudging me out the door.

Sure enough, a light downpour turns torrential as I hang up the last towel, and I put the basket over my head and waddle over to stand under the eaves on the side of the abbey. I lean against the wall to wait for a lull, happy to take a bit more time away from Sister Agnes.

I sit on the dry ground next to the abbey wall. To my left is a row of windows. I hear voices and realize that these windows are right off the abbess's study. There's a soft, distant sound of spoons clinking against teacups. I imagine the abbess putting in her standard three cubes of sugar, the way Sister Bernadette told me she does.

"So, it seems that all your paperwork is in order," she says. "The final step is to tell us a little more about yourselves so we can be sure you're the right fit."

Someone sets a cup down heavily, then murmurs an apology—a man's deep voice. I am trying to remember his face, but all I see is that plaid shirt and possibly a beard. I wish I'd paid better attention.

"I work at the mill in town," he says. "It's good, steady pay and I'll probably get moved to foreman within a couple years."

He has a simple way of talking, but you can hear the kindness in his voice. He seems reluctant, or maybe unpracticed, talking about himself.

His wife jumps in to finish his sentences. "He got employee of the year last year; he's a good worker, super dependable. He's going to go far."

The abbess can tell they're nervous, and she doesn't seem to be the kind of person to make others suffer. "I hope I'm not putting you on the spot," she says. "It's just important to us that this baby have a good home. The mother is not some stranger, she's a member of our own family."

It's the last part of this sentence that hits me. *She's a member of our own family?*

"The doctors have said we can never have kids," the woman says. "We just want a family. We would do everything possible to make sure the baby had a good life."

"If it's a boy I can teach him to hunt—" the man begins, but his wife cuts him off. "We'd love it if it's a girl, as well. Of course, if she wanted to hunt, too . . ." She trails off, and I imagine them looking at each other wondering if hunting was the wrong topic. I doubt the abbess knows what to think, but it makes me smile.

"We just really want a family," the woman says again, a bit defeated, like she's throwing out one last plea into the wind, hoping Mother Superior will catch it.

"Well, there's still a few months before the birth, so we'll get back to you and let you know about your application. I'm sure the Lord knows what's best for everyone," says the abbess.

They shake hands and I hear the abbess say a prayer, asking for God's will and for them to trust in him, and then they leave her office. I stare out at the towels and the rain, wondering if I should go finish up before anyone sees me, but it doesn't seem as important anymore.

I forget sometimes that this pregnancy won't last forever. It will be strange not to feel the baby moving, kicking, swimming around inside me—as much as I didn't want it, it's hard to remember what I was like before. When it's over, I'll have to get used to not knowing anything about my baby.

It's obvious now why all these couples keep visiting, but

why can't they just tell me? It feels exactly like Gran ignoring me for months and then one day putting me on a bus.

Sister Josephine has entered the study. She and the abbess are talking so quietly, I have to lean closer to the window to hear.

"I don't know, they seem a bit young," Mother Superior says.

"Well, they are married, and certainly older than Ruth," says Sister Josephine.

"I just wonder . . . he did seem keen on hunting. What if it is a girl?"

"I'm not sure that's grounds for being a bad parent," says Sister Josephine. "Things are changing, Mother; I think girls can hunt. No disrespect, but you're from a few generations back."

The abbess laughs quietly. "You know, Sister Josephine, maybe I'm not the one who should be making this decision. What experience do I have besides Marguerite, and now Ruth? She wanted me to give Ruth those flowers, but did you notice she had them in a whiskey bottle? Heavens, if that's something this generation thinks is appropriate, then I am truly outdated."

At these words I jump to my feet, or try to. I struggle and pull myself up along the wall. Then, as fast as my body will let me move, I run out to the parking area, just in time to see the lime-green car backing out.

"Stop!"

The man slams on the brakes, looking in his rearview mirror at me standing right behind his car. I am soaking wet, my dress clinging to my round belly, my hair sopping. I must look terrifying.

But the man opens the door and walks around the car. "Are you all right?" he asks me in the kindest voice ever. It reminds me of George back in the Salvation Army, except that this man has steel-blue eyes and a ginger beard. The woman is out of the car now, too, still holding the glass bottle full of bluebells. I stare at the whiskey bottle and feel like I am five years old again; the smell of my parents' house wraps around me as if someone has put a blanket over my wet, wet shoulders. Her hair looks so much like my mother's, after my father twirled his bloody fingers in it and they danced in the kitchen.

"What's your favorite kind of venison?" I hear myself say to the man, who is looking at me the way I'm sure he looks at a deer in the forest. Hesitantly, no sudden movements, so it doesn't bolt and run away. If he thinks the question is odd, he doesn't show it.

"I like the shoulder cut," he says. "But it has to cook all day or it's too tough."

I must look disappointed, because the woman touches his arm lightly and says, "I like backstrap. Everyone knows backstrap is the best cut."

She smiles—a genuine smile.

"Are those flowers really for me?" I ask her.

"They are," she says. Her eyes take in my round stomach, bobbing like a buoy under my wet dress.

She hands me the bottle and it feels heavier than it looks, as if it holds every wildflower bouquet I have missed since my mother left.

I remember Dumpling's voice saying, *"Sometimes you just have to hold on to whatever you can,"* and me saying to Hank, *"You mean, like something to look forward to?"*

"Would you really love my baby?" I ask her.

"With all my heart," she says. "And you, for trusting me."

I stare at the wildflowers spilling out of the whiskey bottle vase, and I know that these are the people that should raise my baby.

I reach inside my pocket for the other half of the red ribbon. I've cut it just like Dumpling told me to.

"Will you give this to my baby?" I hold it out to the woman, who takes it gingerly, like it's the most fragile, beautiful thing she's ever held.

I don't know how long the nuns have been standing outside watching us, their habits getting drenched in the rain. The abbess comes over then and really does place a blanket over my shoulders.

"You don't have to make any decisions," she tells me.

"No," I say, "I do. It's my life. It's my baby. And I want to know that both of us have something good to look forward to."

Right then Sister Agnes surprises us by bursting into tears and fleeing back into the kitchen. Sister Josephine and Sister Bernadette look at me and shake their heads, but they, too, wipe their eyes with the corner of their wet habits. I stare at these women, who used to scare me in their long black robes, flitting around the abbey like bats.

There's Sister Bernadette, who smells of pistachios and always leaves a cup of tea by my bed; Sister Josephine, with her lead foot and the way she's helped me understand Gran; even Sister Agnes, off in the kitchen now, because she has to be gruff or she wouldn't know what to do with herself. I remember the abbess saying *"She's a member of our own family,"* and I remember Selma's letter—how I rolled my eyes at her words even as she knew I would. But once again, Selma was right. *We don't have to be blood to be family.*

CHAPTER FOURTEEN

Blueberry Pie

DORA

Dumpling has been in a coma for weeks now, but she also has a punctured lung and a broken clavicle. Her father might have gotten to her sooner if I hadn't said she was right behind us, but everyone tells me it's not my fault. *No, I think, it's all Ruth's fault.* Ruth and her stupid blue note.

I thought it while I watched them load Dumpling into the plane to be medevaced to Fairbanks; I thought it as we packed up fish camp to return home early; and I'm thinking it now as I bake a blueberry pie because Dumpling's mother asked me to, before she left to go sit beside Dumpling's hospital bed again. She wants me to take it over to the Lawrences', and I wonder if she knows I would rather throw it in their gran's face than give her a pie while my best friend lies silent in a coma. "Damn you straight to hell, Ruth Lawrence," I whisper as I roll out the crust.

It has ruined the smell of blueberries for me, probably forever. Because isn't that how forever happens—instantly? One minute your best friend is right there, and then suddenly she's not. I used to love the smell of sweet, hot blueberries signaling the end of summer. Just the right amount of Crisco flaking the crust, the bubbly berries seeping out onto the oven floor and smoking up the whole house. These berries are from last year's haul on the top of Shotgun Ridge, from a sunny day after Dumpling and Bunny had come home from fish camp and we hiked up to the secret berry spot, up past the tree line where you could see to the end of everywhere. We were all sweating and covered in DEET, but it didn't make any difference to the mosquitoes. We picked until our fingers were solid purple, and Bunny's teeth and lips, too, because she always ate more than she put aside.

It was a bumper crop and a perfect fall day, when everything smells ripe, like it's just about to turn and it's rushing to do so before winter. It's the cry of fall: *Hurry up and fill the buckets; hurry up, the fireweed is about to top off. Once it does, the snow is right around the corner and that's it for another year. Hurry, hurry, hurry.*

If the seasons bleed into each other like a watercolor painting, it means not enough fish and berries to last the winter, not enough wood chopped for the stove, not enough meat in the freezer. One year winter came so fast and so hard, the leaves on the birch trees didn't even have time to turn yellow and fall off; they froze solid green on the branches. They clung there for months on skinny skeleton arms, the color so blindingly wrong it was creepy. Every year it's a race between the seasons, and that year fall lost.

And then it hits me—Dumpling lying in her hospital bed is just like fall. *Wake up, Dumpling, wake up, wake up, it's almost winter, hurry, hurry, hurry,* I whisper to her in my head, praying that somehow she can hear me.

Dumpling's father comes in looking even older than he did when he left this morning to go sit by Dumpling's bed with her mother. I know her condition is still the same or he wouldn't look like he does. I pour him a cup of the brothers and he smiles at me, as if it takes all his strength.

"Pie smells good," he says. "Is that for Lily's gran?"

"Why do I have to take a pie to their gran?" I try not to sound angry. He smiles again, as if my question doesn't surprise him in the least.

"She's an elder," he says simply.

"Yeah, but . . ." Dumpling's dad does not have to yell or throw things the way my dad does to let me know when I've gone too far. The way he looks at me makes me want to crawl under the table.

"There were a bunch of us who worked really hard to defend the rights of all Alaskans," he tells me, and I'm not sure what that has to do with pie.

"We didn't want to become a state; we wanted to continue to have certain freedoms we'd always had. The right to fish and hunt on our own land; to protect our culture. You know, simple human rights, and it wasn't just native—a lot of non-native Alaskans stood right alongside us—all worried about what statehood would mean."

I squirm, thinking about my dad drinking at the bar and letting everyone else do all the heavy lifting.

"I was supposed to be on that plane," Dumpling's dad is saying. "The one that went down in Canada and killed five of my good friends, including Ruth and Lily's dad."

I look down at my purple fingers, stained with berry juice.

"Their mother will never be okay again after losing him, and her gran is trying to raise them all on her own. Is a pie asking too much, Dora?"

"Did you know about the note?" I ask him, trying to keep my voice as steady as possible, trying not to be a disappointment.

"I'm the one who told Dumpling where Ruth's mother is. I visit her from time to time—they hoped seeing a familiar face would jog a part of her memory."

He looks defeated.

"It's my fault, Dora. I shouldn't have let any of you girls go there. Dumpling's accident is all my fault."

He slumps in his seat. Adults never talk to us kids like this and I'm not sure how to respond, but I don't believe it was his fault. Luckily the oven timer dings, and I can busy myself getting the pie out of the oven.

* * *

I knock on the Lawrences' door, balancing the sticky, hot pie on an oven mitt. I hope desperately that Lily will answer, but that would make me a lucky person and that's not how I would describe myself.

I've never been up close to their gran before, and when the door opens I brace myself, expecting to see eyes sunk deep in their sockets and perhaps fangs instead of teeth, so I am surprised when she is nothing but an old woman in a faded flowered housecoat. Her wispy gray hair looks like a dust bunny stuck on her head. I could never throw a pie at someone who looks like she does.

"Hello, Dora," she says. "Won't you come in?"

The kitchen is totally bare, smelling of floor wax and Comet and not a hint of anyone my age or younger possibly living here. I've become so accustomed to Dumpling's house, which is a bustle of activity, with piles of tanned animal skins everywhere waiting to be sewn into hats and mittens, and muddy footprints because who has time to take off their shoes when you just need to grab that book you forgot or one more stick of venison jerky on your way out the door? It smells like a place where people like each other, and the Lawrence house smells like it's judging you the minute you walk inside. I make sure to slide out of my shoes before I step onto the worn, but still shiny, linoleum.

Gran—I don't know what else to call her—motions for me to place the pie on the counter. "That smells wonderful," she says as she opens the refrigerator, pulling out a brown Tupperware pitcher. I am annoyed at the way she seemed to expect the pie.

"Would you like some Tang?"

But she is already pouring me a glass, even though I haven't said anything.

"Here; sit, sit," she says, setting the glass down on the table, which is also polished to a shine and smells of Lemon Pledge. There are no stacks of magazines, or unopened bills, or plates of half-eaten food. There's not even one crumb. It's unlike any table I've ever seen, and I am careful not to spill a drop of orange Tang on it.

She pours herself some coffee and sits across from me.

I take a gulp of what is normally a sickly sweet drink, but this just tastes like orange-flavored water. Either Gran is skimpy with the powder or Bunny is generous when she makes ours.

"Did you know that Dumpling's father was a very close friend of Ruth and Lily's father?" she asks.

I keep my eyes down. Why does everyone keep saying that? Who cares if their father worked for native rights and died in a plane crash? Lots of people die in plane crashes every single day around here.

I do not need to sit here and listen to an old woman who smells like cleaning products talk about dead people. I need to go visit my friend Dumpling and rattle her bones until she wakes up. I push my chair back so hard, it makes a loud screeching sound on her perfect floor and I hope I've marked it up.

Gran looks at me. "You seem angry, Dora."

"I seem angry?" I yell at her, before I can stop myself. "Do you know what Dumpling was doing in that village? Do you know why she was there? It's all Ruth's fault! Dumpling was trying to give Ruth's mother this note."

I slam the blue note down on the table, making her coffee slosh over the rim of her cup. She doesn't even seem to notice as she picks up the blue paper and reads the words that have played in a loop in my brain ever since the day Dumpling thrust the note into my hand. All it says is "I forgive you."

"And that stupid woman didn't even know who Ruth was, so it wouldn't have made a damn bit of difference anyway. Dumpling is in a coma for nothing!" I am out of breath, still shaking.

"Sit down, Dora," she says.

But I don't. I stay standing with my hands clenched. She cannot tell me what to do.

"Okay," she says, "but you should hear me out. If you want to blame someone, and apparently you do, you should blame me—and don't worry, nobody will be risking their life to get a note like this to me, not anytime soon, anyway."

I am worn out from my rant and her words are so quiet, hanging in the air next to mine. It is hard to stay angry when nobody challenges you.

"Still want to stand?"

I sit.

"We have something in common—you and I, Dora," she says. "I see that surprises you."

I shut my mouth, which has fallen open.

She continues, "My father left me when I was a small child."

"I wish we had that in common," I say, and then stop in case she thinks I'm being sassy on top of yelling at her.

But she smiles at me. She is nothing like the stories I heard from Bunny and Lily: a ferocious monster with eyes in the back of her head, waiting to dole out punishment for the smallest infraction.

"Once she made Lily say the whole rosary, on her knees," Bunny said, *"just for hiding peas in her milk glass."*

"You are still young," Gran says, and I have no idea what this has to do with anything. "You've been given a chance to live with a family who loves you. But you have to stop expecting the worst out of life, or believe me, that's just what will happen. You should listen to an old lady who knows."

I feel a tear and wipe it away. But there's another one right behind it, and soon too many to stop, so I don't try. I cannot remember the last time I cried. Now I worry that I will drown right here in the Lawrences' kitchen. Gran hands me a box of tissues.

"I know," she says, patting my hand. "I know."

She just leaves me to it. I can hear her moving around in the kitchen, getting plates out of the cupboard and clinking the silverware. Soon she brings me a piece of pie and some more watery Tang, and I manage to blow my nose and mumble a feeble thanks.

"I think it's too late for me to change much about my life," she says, "but you still have a chance."

* * *

I think of the poem about the girl in the magenta pinafore and the woman named Rita dancing the cha-cha in her swishy black dress. So, this is what chopping open your body feels like. It's just admitting to yourself what you've always wanted. And there it is, sitting inside my rib cage like a key in a lock, just waiting to be turned.

"I want to know that I can stay in Dumpling's family and never have to go home," I tell her, as if wanting something for myself is as simple as saying it out loud. "I want to be able to sleep at night," I add, poking at the pie crust with my fork, saying too much.

"I think that sounds reasonable," Gran says.

How could someone this nice have sent her granddaughter away?

Her smile fades and I wonder if maybe I said that out loud, or she really is a mind reader like Bunny and Lily say.

First Dumpling's dad and now this. I have no idea how to respond, but it doesn't matter anyway because just then Bunny and Lily come barging through the door, chanting at the top of their lungs, "Dumpling's awake, Dumpling's awake, Dumpling's awake!"

And then we are all hugging and laughing. Gran wraps each of us in turn in her wobbly arms, wiping her eyes with the hem of her dress, and even Bunny seems surprised. I look at Ruth's note still lying on the table, the words *I forgive you* smudged and blurry.

I slip the note into my pocket without anyone noticing, just in case Ruth might want to have it back someday.

I am skipping back over to Dumpling's with Bunny and Lily at my heels, all of us floating with happiness, lighter than we've been in weeks, when suddenly screams and crashing sounds from inside my mother's house stop us in our tracks. We are halfway between Lily's door and my old house, trapped like ptarmigan between two hunters, when the door flies open and Mom's friends Paula and Annette appear, looking terrified.

"Your dad," Paula says, looking right at me. "You girls get away."

"Where's my mom?" I ask, surprised by how calm my voice sounds. My arms are extended, covering Bunny and Lily who are cowering behind me.

"She's hurt," Annette says. I have never seen Annette not laughing. She looks panicked.

"Are you leaving her in there with him?" I ask.

They are pushing each other down the porch, trying to get away. "Wait, you just left her?" I say again. If Paula and Annette are running away, then something very serious is going on inside that house.

I whisper to Bunny to walk slowly backward with Lily and go back to Gran's. Glancing behind me, I see Gran in the doorway and she locks her eyes with mine in agreement— signaling the girls to come back. I can't believe we were just laughing and hugging.

"Tell her to call the police," I tell Bunny, who stares at me as if I am speaking Japanese. "GO, BUNNY. NOW!"

"Dora?" she says. Bunny knows better than to call the police.

"Tell Gran I said to call them; just do it," I tell her. They make it back to the steps of Gran's house just as my father staggers out onto the porch.

"Look at the little rabbits—pow, pow, pow," my dad says, and my heart sinks as I notice he is holding a real hunting rifle, pretending to shoot at the girls. At least Gran has quickly pulled them inside, and he is probably too drunk to hit them from this distance anyway. Paula and Annette are crouched down on the far side of the merry-go-round, which is as far away as they could get.

But I am much, much closer.

"Where is Mom?" I hear myself say.

"Where is Mom?" he mimics in a high-pitched voice. "Oh, someone cares about Mom suddenly, does she?" He waves the rifle in the air as he talks.

I am strangely calm, now that Bunny and Lily are out of sight. Perhaps it was my conversation with Gran, or that I am all cried out, or that Dumpling is awake. Whatever the reason, I am not sliding back into that familiar place of dread and fear.

My father standing on the porch with a rifle does not scare me as much as all the nights I lay awake wondering what he might do to me. At least now I know what I'm dealing with—a drunk man with a gun—not something in the dark that I can't defend myself against: the smell of alcohol on hot, putrid breath coming closer and closer as I hide my head under my pillow and wait for groping hands—so drunk they cannot even remember what they did the next morning.

A rifle is nothing compared to that.

"You're going to give me that money, Dora," he says, but his voice sounds less dangerous in the light of day and I can tell he thinks so, too.

"Fine," I say. "But let me make sure Mom is okay first."

"*Fine,*" he says, repeating every word again in that high-pitched mocking voice.

In the distance I hear a faint siren. *Thank you, Gran,* I think. I just need to hold on a little longer. But he hears the siren, too, and another one, and another one. They are getting louder.

"You little snitch," he says to me. "You had those baby rabbits do your dirty work for you—you goddamn snitch." A snitch. The worst possible thing a person can be around here. He holds the gun up and looks at me through the sight.

"Shoot me," I say. I am not quivering. I am not even scared. "Shoot me so I never have to see your face again."

He is so surprised he just stands there, lowering the gun and trying to figure out who I am. The police cars pull up and park at crazy angles, spraying dust and gravel everywhere. "Drop the rifle and put your hands up," they shout from behind the doors of their patrol cars. My father drops the gun, but he keeps staring at me. They approach from all sides, then rush up, guns drawn, and handcuff him. The whole time we never stop staring at each other. I hope it's the last time I ever have to look into those red, bloodshot eyes.

They load him into the back of a police car and the siren wails again, this time in the other direction, and I realize I've been holding my breath.

Dumpling's dad appears just as all the tension that had been holding me together leaks out of me. He has to prop me up because my legs give out.

"Are you okay?" he says.

I've never seen so much love and concern on the face of anyone. At least not for me. "Can I stay with your family? Can I stay and never have to leave?" I whisper, barely able to find my voice.

"Oh Dora, you don't have to ask," he says, wrapping me in his huge arms.

The paramedics appear from inside the house with my mom strapped to a stretcher. She is black and blue, her arm is in a sling, and her eyes are swollen shut. "Mom?" I say.

"Dora, no hospital," she says. "Tell them—we don't go to hospital."

"It's okay," I tell her. "I'll pay. You look terrible."

"She's got a concussion," says one of the paramedics. "We need to watch her."

"I'm not going to stand by and pretend he didn't hurt you," I say, realizing that's what I have always wanted her to say to me.

Paula and Annette tell the paramedics they're riding along

in the ambulance and won't take no for an answer. Nobody expects me to come, too, which is good because I have someone more important to see right now anyway.

"Is Dumpling up for visitors?" I ask her dad.

"Only if it's you," he says.

CHAPTER FIFTEEN

Bun Heads

HANK

I badly want to talk to Isabelle, but she is acting strange all of a sudden, as if she just drove two thousand miles to watch girls flounce around in tights. It's not even a performance; it's an audition, which means people aren't sitting in seats waiting for the show. Instead there are long-legged ballerinas in tutus milling about everywhere, waiting for their turn.

When we step inside there is nowhere to put your eyes because wherever you look feels wrong.

Isabelle checks the schedule and says, "We might be too late," then rushes down to the side stage door, gesturing for us to follow. We almost knock over a bony woman with wild salt-and-pepper hair standing just inside the door, but before she can topple over, Isabelle grabs her and they hug, whispering frantically to us that this is Abigail and we can all talk afterward. At the last second, a girl with big brown eyes runs up and Abigail smiles at her, saying, "Honey, you're going to miss it, hurry up," as she, too, steps inside and the lights dim.

The auditorium appears mostly empty, but it's too dark to see anything except shadows and outlines. We're backstage, so Abigail motions for us to peer through the thick velvet curtains. All I can see are the judges in the front row, their glasses perched on the ends of beaky noses. This must be a very big deal. You can feel the tension and the judges are the serious unsmiling kind, which is never a good sign.

The girl standing onstage is waiting for her cue. *That's Abigail's niece,* Isabelle mouths silently at me. We did just barely make it in time.

She is long and lean like every other dancer, in a simple pink skirt and white tights, her hands held in front of her, fingertips touching. She looks like a wax statue on display. It's stifling hot. I imagine her melting drip by drip onto the stage. But then I remember I'm still wearing two jackets, so maybe it's only sweltering for me.

I wonder if Jack is sweating, too. He's slipped off to the side and into one of the aisle seats next to the girl Abigail had called "honey." The music starts and the ballerina onstage moves as if pulled by an invisible string. She's mesmerizing, sliding across the stage like butter, leaping and landing very lightly on the tip of one toe, determination written all over her face. She is not just dancing, she is telling the judges a story, and it feels urgent. I lean forward, afraid of missing a single word.

When the music stops I barely notice. Abigail's niece is bowing in front of the judges and I am twisting the red ribbon around and around on my wrist, thinking of a pregnant girl I'd sat next to on a riverbank.

I push past Isabelle and Abigail, who are still clapping, and slam my way through the double stage doors, not caring that I knock a couple of bun heads out of the way. I rip off one of my jackets and storm toward the exits. I just need air.

"Hank," Jack calls through the crowd, "Hank, guess who this is?" He is pointing at the brown-eyed girl, but then a sea of people push past and Jack is swallowed up by more bun heads and tutus.

The room grows blurry. Jack keeps calling my name, but I need to find an exit.

I've turned the wrong way again, back toward the hallway that led backstage. I'm like a rat in a maze. Another exit sign appears up ahead, but just before I reach it, a hand grabs the bottom of my jacket from behind. "Hank," says Jack. "Stop."

The girl beside him is holding the paper towel with the name "Selma" on it in Phil's thick, black handwriting. I stare at the letters, remembering how Jack traced them all the way across the Yukon. Of course they would lead straight to a real live girl, if for no other reason than Jack believed they would. She is looking at him with brown mud-puddle eyes, and they are shimmering, as if he holds all the answers to the universe.

"This is Selma," Jack whispers.

We all just stand there staring at each other.

Until the backstage doors fly open and four people walk out. Isabelle, Abigail, the ballerina, and . . .

"I KNEW IT," Jack cries. "SAM, I KNEW YOU WERE ALIVE!"

CHAPTER SIXTEEN

Brothers

ALYCE

I didn't even have time to catch my breath. One minute Sam was there, handing me a bouquet of roses as we exited through the side stage doors, and the next minute he was on the ground with another boy on top of him.

Aunt Abigail and a woman I'd never seen before were blowing their noses into hankies, and Selma was standing there looking like she'd just stepped off a fast-moving train. Then Mom came running out from stage left, skipping toward me with more flowers and saying, "You were wonderful." But then she stopped, taking in the commotion all around us.

Off to the side, another boy was slumped down against the wall with his head in his hands. Everyone seemed to notice him at the same moment. Sam disentangled himself from the first and went over to the other one, who was older, sadder, and more disheveled. Sam kneeled, burying his head in the boy's shoulder. The words he'd been mumbling grew louder and louder as Sam hugged him: "I thought you were dead, I thought you were dead, I thought you were dead."

Jack. Hank. It was like walking from a dark room into bright sunlight. My eyes kept trying to adjust, unable to focus on seeing these three brothers, all finally together.

And just when Sam had started to lose faith that he would actually find them.

"It's beginning to feel like a needle in a haystack," he'd said, as soon as we were back in Fairbanks. Mom was overly excited to have us and had made her famous lasagna for a "welcome home" meal. Afterward as we cleaned up in the kitchen, she stressed that Sam could stay as long as he needed to.

"I've heard so much about you," she told him.

"You have?" I asked.

"Oh Alyce, it's not as if your father and I never talk."

"You do?"

But she just swatted me playfully like I was kidding around.

"My sister works at the paper," she told Sam. "If your brothers are in Fairbanks, she'll be the first to know."

He smiled and thanked her, but when she went back out to the dining room for more dirty plates, it was obvious his smile hadn't been real.

I can tell what Sam's feeling by the shadows that flit across his face; the way his eyes flash many shades of brown, like a spinning kaleidoscope, especially when he is thinking about his brothers.

"Aunt Abigail is on it," I told him. "She's a great reporter and she knows everything and everyone. Really, she'll find them."

He'd moved forward and draped the dish towel he was holding around my shoulders, pulled me right up to his face, and kissed me. I'd been waiting for that kiss for weeks, but it still caught me off guard. I didn't know what to do with my soapy hands, so I ran them through his hair and kissed him back—hard. Just like I'd wanted to so many times before, on the flying bridge, in the *Pelican,* even covered in blood in the troll pit. "Salt," he murmured. "I knew you'd taste salty."

Apparently all of this caught my mother off guard, too, as she came barreling into the kitchen with another stack of plates that flew out of her arms, crashing to the floor and scaring the living daylights out of all of us.

I'm so busy remembering that kiss, I barely feel the tug on my arm pulling me back to the auditorium hallway. In front of me on the red flowered carpet, Sam and Hank are still holding on to each other. I can feel my mascara running down my cheeks.

"Hi," says a blurry face pressing close to mine.

"Jack?"

The face nods.

"Did Sam give you that?" He points to the red rubber band sticking out from where I tried to hide it under my bun.

"He did."

"Did you know it's lucky?" he asks.

"That's why I'm wearing it."

"Did you save him?"

"I tried," I say. "Maybe he saved me?"

"Yeah, that's what we do, isn't it?" Jack says. "We save each other."

"You're exactly how he described you," I tell him, and he grins.

"You were amazing," Selma says, stepping closer to Jack and me. Her smile is unlike anything I've ever seen on Selma's face before. "Your audition, Alyce . . . it was perfect. You are definitely going to get in." She's holding a crumpled paper towel with her name on it and looks funny—punch-drunk.

"Thanks . . . what's that?" I ask. She's cradling it almost the same way I'm holding the bouquet of roses from Sam.

She presses it close to her chest, as if it's a love letter. "Just something I've been waiting for all my life."

I can't wrap my mind around what's made Selma act so un-Selma-like—normally it's impossible to get her to stop talking—but nothing makes sense right now and my legs are cramping up. I need to go stretch but the emotion in the hallway is so thick, it would be easier to cut through the neck bone of a salmon than walk past all these people. Sam is whispering in Hank's ear. Maybe he's telling him the story of the orcas, and how he ended up here?

Sam must look so different to his brothers. I'm sure he's changed a lot since they last saw him. My mother bought the clothes he's wearing at Sears Roebuck two weeks ago, when we first arrived in Fairbanks, because all he had were Uncle Gorky's old ones. I'm still getting used to seeing him in them myself.

Even when we first got here for the audition—was that just a few hours ago?—he seemed so out of place. Stiff, and more seasick than he ever looked on the boat. He gestured at my pointe shoes. "They look so weird on your feet."

I thought so, too. "They'd look weird anywhere but hanging over the bunk during fishing season."

Maybe he thought I still felt guilty, because he said, "Your dad doesn't want you to live your life trying to please him. He really wants you to be happy."

And then he leaned back in case that made me mad like it did the last time he'd said that.

But I get it now. I'd thought I was protecting my dad all this time, but I'm pretty sure he's always just wanted me to be me.

For the first time, I danced like someone who knew what she wanted. It felt fearless, like I was letting nobody down, especially myself.

But even that doesn't seem quite as important now, watching Hank and Sam. He was wrong about Hank being mad at him, or not worried. I add up every minute, hour, and day I spent with Sam, and it's obvious that every one of them Hank spent thinking Sam was dead. I feel selfish, watching Hank try to come back from such a dark, dark place. I'm not sure I would ever stop crying if I were him.

"I had a feeling," Jack says suddenly, watching me closely, "that there was someone like you out there with him."

He hugs me.

"You were right," I tell him. "Will Hank be okay?"

"Hank's fine," Jack says. "Or he will be."

Jack has Sam's eyes.

I'm so busy noticing Jack that I don't realize Hank and Sam are no longer sitting on the floor until I feel a hand on my shoulder.

"Alyce, this is Hank," Sam says. It seems impolite to stare at Hank's tear-stained face and red, puffy cheeks. But he steps forward and hugs me, squishing the roses between us. He smells like miles and miles of mud-soaked road, mingled with sweat and a hint of lavender; beneath it all is the familiar musty smell of a boat. He gives me a squeeze, then steps back and says, "You're a beautiful dancer. It almost killed me watching you."

Even though I'm not sure I understand exactly what he means, I know it's one of the nicest things anyone has ever said to me.

WINTER

The earth is frozen
All around our garbage cans
Raven tracks in frost.

—JOHN STRALEY

CHAPTER SEVENTEEN

December 1970

RUTH

Even after your heart breaks into a million pieces and your baby is gone, I am here to tell you—all around you the world will still go on spinning. People might even say kind words to you and think you are listening, but mostly you won't hear anything because you're too busy collecting each of those tiny pieces of your heart—wrapping them up into a safe corner of yourself, so you can find them again later.

You might only be able to nod at first, at the smiling faces that look familiar, and the mouths with the silent words trying to tell you something. It could be a while before you realize what they're saying.

And then, on a morning like any other morning, you'll start to wiggle your toes. Or feel the blood returning to the tips of your fingers. Slowly, like warmth after frost nip. All that new blood will seep back into those frozen spots until it reaches the secret place where you've hidden all the broken pieces—shards, really—and you start to move them around, maybe fit them back into place. Although you probably won't get them exactly the way they were before, so it will feel funny at first and you might have to do it a few times.

Slowly, slowly, you'll start to do normal things, like drink a cup of tea that will taste like tea again, instead of just brown water that someone has thrust into your hands for no reason. Things like taste and smell and touch—they'll all come back, but slowly.

"It just takes time," you'll hear over and over again, once you can hear again.

When you do decide to speak, you limit yourself to asking only one question a day, at least in the beginning.

Day One:
  "Was it a boy or a girl?"
  "It was a beautiful, healthy little girl." (Sister Bernadette)

Day Two:
  "What did they name her?"
  "You don't remember? You asked that they name her after your gran. Marguerite." (Sister Josephine)

Day Three:
  "Why did I name her after my gran?" I really can't remember.

"I think you were trying to wipe the slate clean—a new beginning." (the abbess)

After two or three weeks, people will expect you to think about getting on with your life, especially Sister Agnes. Eventually you will say good-bye and push out through the abbey gates, trying not to hear the sniffling nuns behind you. You won't be the same girl who walked up the steps of that exact same bus all those months ago even though you are wearing the same ratty red coat and carrying the same brown satchel. You'll watch the world go quickly by, as if it's a movie being played in reverse. The hours and then the days come and go before you barely even blink. You think maybe it's been five days because Sister Agnes gave you enough sandwiches and scones for at least a week, and the last few have begun to taste old and dry, like sawdust. The only thing anchoring you to your seat is the embroidered pillow you found stuffed into your satchel, a gift from Sister Josephine and Sister Bernadette. You clutch it with both hands and bury your face in the stitches, breathing in the smell of the nuns, trying not to float away completely. Until you recognize the truck stop where you bought an apple pie for your seventeenth birthday, but you were not alone then and you are now.

Except for the stranger who leans over and says, "Can I ask you something?"

"Me?"

He looks around. "We're the only two people on this bus," he says.

The spell is broken. I am a person, back in my old body.

I look into his eyes, which are a funny shade of green, like beach glass washed up on the shore. His face is weathered, so it's impossible to tell his age.

"So, I was wondering," he says, "I'm going to meet someone for the first time and she's about your age. I'm nervous about the gift I got her."

I wonder how old he thinks I am. I could be seventeen or seventy; I don't know how much my outside matches my insides anymore.

But he's busy riffling through his backpack and pulls out two bars of homemade soap. "Soap?" I say, and I can tell he was hoping for more enthusiasm. "I mean, wow, soap," I say again. He laughs a deep, barrel-chested laugh that warms up the empty bus.

"A friend of mine made it," he says. "I thought teenage girls liked things like baths and . . . stuff."

"No, really, she'll love the soap," I tell him, and he hands me a bar. It smells like lemons. "I lived with some . . . uh, women . . . who made soap," I say, the longest sentence I've uttered in weeks.

He doesn't press me to say more. I hand him back the soap and then curl up on the seat pretending to read.

Outside the bus windows, the sky is turning pink; the sun is already setting even though it's only two in the afternoon.

There is nothing but miles and miles of mountainous terrain reminding me that I am just a tiny speck in the universe.

The next time I wake, there are a few more people on board. Mostly men, and I wonder what I must look like, a young girl traveling alone at Christmas. Soap guy is talking about fishing and boats with a man who must have got on near the border. The new guy has a dry bag sitting on the seat next to him that smells like diesel, mildew, and fish.

Selma's most recent letter falls out of my book. I forgot that I stashed it there, a few weeks ago when the words failed to make any sense to me.

Selma says she finally learned the truth about where she came from, but she can only do the story justice in person— she can't wait to tell me. Her cousin, Alyce, has been accepted to a college dance program; there's a bunch of new boys in town attracting all sorts of attention; and, most perplexing, Dora and Dumpling (who has recovered slowly from her accident) spend a lot of time at my house, with Lily and Bunny.

I want to hear Selma's story and I want to see Lily and Dumpling, but beyond that I haven't let myself think much about going back.

The abbess did say Gran would meet me at the bus station. I wonder if she'll pretend nothing's happened and act like she did before—because I'm not the same person I was before. And I doubt I can see her the same way, either, after everything Sister Josephine's told me.

It makes me so tired just thinking about Gran that I fall

back to sleep, Selma's letter fresh on my mind, the smell of that man's dry bag filling my nose.

I dream I am sitting on the edge of the ocean. The moon is shining, and I can see huge rocks bobbing into view as the tide goes out, and the beach is suddenly full of starfish and small crabs scurrying away under the moonlight. Something is sitting on the rock and I see it is a woman; she has dropped her clothes into a pile. She leaves them on the rock and comes to the beach, stepping gingerly over broken shells and seaweed. She walks right past me but doesn't see me; she's heading to the harbor where the boats are tied up, lights shining inside their wheelhouses. My curiosity draws me to the rock. What I thought were clothes is a wet, shiny sealskin, reeking of rancid fish. The skin is oily and slips from my grasp into the ocean. I watch in horror as it starts to float away and I can't grab on to it—I'm swimming and swimming, and if I don't save it that woman will never be able to go back to the sea, but I can't reach it.

Crash!

I wake up on the floor of the bus.

"Sorry, everybody—moose in the road," says the driver, who slammed on the brakes. "We'll be in Fairbanks in about fifteen minutes."

"Are you okay?" asks stinky dry-bag guy as I pull myself up off the floor.

I nod, but my coat is wet and splotched with mud and dirty snow melted from people's boots. He turns back to talk to soap guy.

"I have to buy some roses," he says. "I've been warned by

my ex-wife that if I show up at *The Nutcracker* without roses, I may as well not show up at all."

Soap guy laughs and says, "I hear that's where I'm headed, too."

It's the last thing I'd expect from either one of them.

The bus pulls into the station garage, where the lights are blinding and it's hard to make out the faces of the people waiting on the curb. Everyone looks a tiny bit different. There is Alyce in full stage makeup, looking shockingly out of place. She's wearing a sparkling tiara and a puffy down coat over her *Nutcracker* costume.

From inside the bus, I watch her throw her arms around the dry-bag guy as he steps onto the curb. Alyce pulls on the arm of a boy—a handsome boy—who comes forward and shakes hands with the guy. I've never seen him before, and I've never seen Alyce's eyes shine like that, either.

My feet have stopped working. The universe is moving at a much faster pace than I'm used to. It's loud and colorful, after months of living in a black-and-white world with whispering nuns, so I take my time getting off the bus. It's easier, watching from this side of the window anyway, until I get my bearings.

Selma's face pops up in the crowd. Not the boisterous Selma I remember—the one who lines up first to get a shot in the arm, or throws back her head and laughs like a hyena— but a hesitant Selma, who is walking shyly toward the soap guy. He's just stepped off the bus with his bag full of lemony soaps slung jauntily over his shoulder.

He holds out a wide hand for her to shake, but she

surprises him (and me) by launching herself straight at him. I've never seen so much hugging in all my life. *So I'm not the reason Selma's here,* I realize as she pulls out another lumpy orange hat and presents it to him as if it's the goose that laid the golden egg. Poor Selma—the biggest heart in the world doesn't make a whit of difference for her knitting. And suddenly I'm laughing—still on the bus, all by myself, laughing. It feels so good.

Until I see Gran—way off on the side of the crowd. She looks older, her hair thinner. In her threadbare overcoat and nylon stockings, she must be freezing. She does not look angry or scary, just nervous and cold. Selma is walking over to her, proudly dragging the soap guy by the arm. Gran shakes his huge hand in her frail little one. It makes her look even smaller—she is shrinking with every minute I don't get off this bus.

It's time I rejoin the world.

I finally stand to leave, when I see him.

Hank.

He is watching someone with that same expression he had the day I saw him watch his brother Jack eat a pink Sno Ball. I follow his gaze, and of course, there's Jack. He's smiling at Selma and the soap guy as if he created them out of thin air. The handsome boy with Alyce is there, too; now he's shaking soap guy's hand and it all looks so cozy—but also impossible for me to reach.

As I think this, Hank glances up and sees me through the window.

He walks slowly toward the bus. Slow enough that I have time to replay our entire last meeting in my mind. By the time he stands at the door of the bus, I have once again seen him naked with a bouquet of bluebells, and draped in a white sheet sitting on a clump of cranberries, saying, *"Maybe I can see you in Fairbanks someday?"*

Now I am standing two steps above him, and apparently this is "someday."

"It's you," he says.

"It's me," I say. For the second time in the span of a week, I have used the word *me*.

I still exist.

But then his brother Jack is beside him, staring at me.

"It's you," he says.

I decide not to say it again.

Then Selma appears and the spell is again broken, at least for now, because she is yelling, "Ruth! You're back! You're back!"

She is genuinely happy to see me, and I feel warmth seep all the way down to my toes as she hugs the air out of me. I hug her back.

She kisses my cheek and whispers, "I missed you."

"I've missed you, too."

At some point I know she'll tell me everything—and it will be worth hearing. For now they will all have to wait—even Hank—until I get past this first reunion with Gran.

But before I can take another step, Hank grabs my wrist and ties the red ribbon onto it. For a split second everything goes quiet, and all I know is that wherever she is, my baby's fat little wrist is wrapped in the other half of this ribbon.

I hear Dumpling's voice saying, *"It works, I promise."*

And I finally understand.

Hank is watching me closely. I point to Gran and say, "You might have to hold the space just a tiny bit longer."

He squeezes my wrist and says, "I'm quite good at waiting."

It feels as if Gran is miles and miles away, rather than just a few yards. She is even frailer up close. I'm not the only one who's aged over the past few months.

"Hi," I say.

She looks like she's going to cry.

"Where's Lily?" I ask, because she seems lost for words.

"She's home baking you a cake."

Then she adds, "Dora and Dumpling and Bunny are there, too. So I hope you're in the mood for a party."

"I named her after you," I blurt out as fast as I can. If I don't say it now, I might never say it.

"I don't deserve that," she says.

"I thought it might be like a do-over," I say, and at first the old Gran looks back at me; her eyes narrow like I've insulted her. And then all of a sudden she laughs—not a deep, rolling laugh like Selma's savior on the bus, but a dry, cobwebby one.

She hugs me tight, even tighter than Selma did, but the smell of her takes me by surprise.

They're the same old smells: Lemon Pledge, Joy soap, and Hills Bros. coffee all jumbled together. But there's one that catches me totally off guard. It's the face cream that Gran has used every morning for as long as I've known her.

"Sister Josephine's milk-and-honey lotion," I say.

It's the smell of two worlds colliding.

She kisses me on the top of my head, like we share a secret.

"I've never been very good with words," she says. "I'm so sorry, Ruth."

Now she really is crying. But so am I.

We link arms and I steer her across the icy sidewalk toward home. It suddenly dawns on me that there is a big difference between feeling tired and being weak. I place my hand on my chest one last time before we reach Birch Park, just to check.

It's still there—my own heart, cobbled together and a little worse for wear—but it's definitely not all beat out.

ACKNOWLEDGMENTS

This book is a work of fiction, but it's also only possible because four generations of one family have lived in one particular place for a very long time. I cannot thank the members of that family enough, every single one of them.

Mainly this started out as a free write in the home of my dear friend and talented writer, Lisa Jones. If Lisa Jones says "Let's all write for twenty minutes about the smell of other people's houses," by all means, do it. *Take a writing class from Lisa Jones if at all possible* is probably the best advice I can ever give anyone.

I wrote a very different version of this book as my creative thesis while attending Hamline University's MFAC program in Writing for Children and Young Adults. I want to thank all of the Hamline faculty, staff, and students, but especially the comma goddess, Marsha Wilson Chall, who was the first person to think this idea had any merit at all.

Claire Rudolph Murphy convinced me that it's not cliché to write about the place you know best, even if it is Alaska (something she does so well herself).

And the incredible Kelly Easton worked so hard on this book that sometimes I still hear her voice in my head saying things like "This is very dark, even for you." Thank you for everything,

Kelly—especially for convincing me that the title should be *The Smell of Other People's Houses.*

My early, early readers won't even recognize what this book has finally become, and I'm sure they'll be pleased about that. Thanks to William DeArmond, one of my dearest, smartest friends, who read it in its infancy and then again in its old age; to the brilliant Nathanael Johnson, who also reminds me a little bit of Jack; and to the amazing Hawaiian filmmaker Anne Keala Kelly, who doesn't mince words and who keeps me on track about all things indigenous.

Rebecca Grabill and Elizabeth Schoenfeld, thanks for a wonderful writing retreat at Bald Head Island in North Carolina (and in Frisco, Colorado, Elizabeth) and for teaching me how to use Scrivener. Thanks to Anne Schwab for opening your cabin in Minnesota to me and to Jodi Baker for giving us weary writers a tour of your apple orchard. Much of this book was written at the Abbey of St. Walburga in Colorado, a place filled with ranching nuns who inspire me.

The Alaska poets who so graciously allowed me to use their poems—John Straley, Nancy White Carlstrom, and Ann Chandonnet—I cannot thank you enough. I have admired all of you for years.

I am indebted to my Athabascan and Inupiat friends who gave me permission to fictionalize aspects of their stories. I understand why you want to remain anonymous but admire and respect everything you do and all you've taught me.

Thank you, Nellie Moore, for reading and for being so patient with me for so many years. Now *get back to work*!

To my agent, Molly Ker Hawn, with whom I knew I wanted to work the minute she tweeted about catching her hair on fire while out to dinner with her in-laws. You are a ball of fire yourself, and I am so thrilled that you never gave up on this book. Or me.

Alice Swan, my lovely, lovely editor at Faber and Faber. Without you, most of the characters in this book would have perished in the Alaskan landscape. You were right that there is more hope in the world than I can sometimes see, but I will keep looking. The entire Faber crew, including Hannah Love, Grace Gleave, Sarah Savitt, and Rebecca Lewis-Oakes, has been just marvelous. Apologies to anyone I may be forgetting; many thanks to you all.

Wendy Lamb and Dana Carey, thank you for the hours and hours you spent on this with so much emotion and energy and the undying belief that it could become what it was supposed to become; and thank you to everyone else at Random House for your care and enthusiasm, especially copy editors Ellen Lind and Colleen Fellingham, designer Trish Parcell, and readers Alexandra Borbolla, Sarah Eckstein, Teria Jennings, Elena Meuse, Makenna Sidle, Alexandra West, and Hannah Weverka. Wendy, thank you for opening your door for us in New York and for keeping it open throughout this whole process.

Ray Shappell, thank you for the gorgeous Random House cover—you nailed it.

Lori Roth Adams, without your Christmas card I would have forgotten about the importance of fishing charts—but never do I underestimate the importance of friends.

Chris Todd, thank you for bringing me coffee in bed every single morning, even when I didn't deserve it, and for reading way too many drafts (even the ones you said you read but only skimmed).

Most of all, to Dylan and Sylvia—millions and millions of mallards to the two people who save me over and over again every single day.

ABOUT THE AUTHOR

Bonnie-Sue Hitchcock was born and raised in Alaska. She worked many years fishing commercially with her family and as a reporter for Alaska Public Radio stations around the state. She was also the host and producer of "Independent Native News," a daily newscast produced in Fairbanks, focusing on Alaska Natives, American Indians, and Canada's First Nations. *The Smell of Other People's Houses* is her first novel.